THE HERO SHE CRAVES

UNBROKEN HEROES
BOOK 3

ANNA HACKETT

The Hero She Craves

Published by Anna Hackett

Cover by Hang Le Designs

Cover image by Wander Aguiar

Edits by Tanya Saari

ISBN (ebook): 978-1-923134-19-5

ISBN (paperback): 978-1-923134-20-1

WHAT READERS ARE SAYING ABOUT ANNA'S ACTION ROMANCE

The Powerbroker - Romantic Book of the Year (Ruby) winner 2022

Heart of Eon - Romantic Book of the Year (Ruby) winner 2020

Cyborg - PRISM Award Winner 2019

Unfathomed and Unmapped - Romantic Book of the Year (Ruby) finalists 2018

Unexplored – Romantic Book of the Year (Ruby) Novella Winner 2017

Return to Dark Earth – One of Library Journal's Best E-Original Books for 2015 and two-time SFR Galaxy Awards winner

At Star's End – One of Library Journal's Best E-Original Romances for 2014

The Phoenix Adventures – SFR Galaxy Award Winner for Most Fun New Series and "Why Isn't This a Movie?" Series

Beneath a Trojan Moon – SFR Galaxy Award Winner and RWAus Ella Award Winner

Hell Squad – SFR Galaxy Award for best Post-Apocalypse for Readers who don't like Post-Apocalypse

"Like Indiana Jones meets Star Wars. A treasure hunt with a steamy romance." – SFF Dragon, review of *Among Galactic Ruins*

"Action, danger, aliens, romance – yup, it's another great book from Anna Hackett!" – Book Gannet Reviews, review of *Hell Squad: Marcus*

Sign up for my VIP mailing list and get your *free box set* containing three action-packed romances.

Visit here to get started: www.annahackett.com

CHAPTER ONE

He strode across the deck of the ship, scanning the gear, the crew, and equipment.

As expected, everything was in order.

Lorenzo "Ren" Santoro crossed his arms over his chest. He hadn't expected anything less. Being second in command of the research vessel *Atalanta* was a job he relished. He'd always loved being on the water. The Navy had ignited that love, and becoming a Navy SEAL had deepened it.

Right now, the ship was in port in San Diego. He liked it most when they were at sea. Surrounded by miles and miles of ocean as far as a man could see. No one, and nothing, to bother him.

He headed down the staircase, boots *thunking* on the metal.

"Hey, Ren," a crew member called out. Like Ren, the man was wearing the ship's uniform—tan cargo pants, and a dark-blue polo shirt with the ship's logo on it—a circle with a crashing wave inside it.

"Everything ready for our guests, Rob?" Ren asked.

"Yes. The cabins and staterooms have been cleaned, the storage area is ready for their gear, and the main lab is all set up."

"Good work." Ren slapped the man's shoulder. He walked past the built-in crane at the back of the ship, then the submersibles strapped down to the deck.

The *Atalanta* was a hell of a research vessel. Owned and funded by a billionaire dedicated to ocean research, they had some of the best crew he'd ever worked with, and all the gear and equipment they needed.

They were currently docked in the Port of San Diego, waiting for their latest clients—a combined team of scientists that were working on a naval project. The hush-hush project was sponsored by the Office of Naval Research, but the scientists were civilians from the Scripps Institution of Oceanography.

The project was classified. No doubt some sort of new tech that the Navy was testing.

Ren had high-level clearance, since he'd initially been a Navy SEAL, but then after that, he'd been recruited into the covert Ghost Ops program. Only the best of the best of the special forces in the country had been invited to join. His former commander, Vander Norcross, was a legend.

He paused, his hands on his hips. Some of the missions had been...rough. They'd been sent into some of the worst places on the planet, to do the seemingly most impossible missions.

For years, he'd thrived on that. On taking risks, challenging himself, on outrunning his past.

But then he'd learned he wasn't invincible.

He shook his head. That part of his life was over. He'd retired several years ago, and figured he'd do something like working private security. But it had turned out that he'd needed something different. Working on the *Atalanta* suited him best.

Ren scanned the ship again, then his gaze shifted out over the water to the horizon. Memories were flitting around in his head today, it seemed. He wouldn't even be here, standing on the deck, if it wasn't for the military. The military had saved his life. He'd grown up with no father. He'd had his mom and *abuela*, but even they hadn't been enough to stop his slow slide into trouble.

He'd been an angry teenager, looking to prove himself.

It hadn't been until he'd met Tom Bradshaw that his life had changed.

"Ren?" another crew member called down from one of the upper decks. "Chef is losing his shit. Says he didn't get all the supplies he ordered."

Ren sighed. Their temperamental Russian chef loved to complain, about everything. Thankfully, the man could cook. "I'll talk to him, Fredrik."

Fredrik looked relieved. "Good luck."

Ren crossed the deck, part of his brain automatically cataloging and checking that everything was in place. His thoughts turned back to this newest project. They would be setting sail in the morning. This afternoon, they'd get the Naval team settled, and their gear stowed. Ren also wanted to make sure the main lab was set up to their specifications. The ship had a hydro lab too if the team required it.

Captain Shroff was planning their route to Hawaii. It would take them five days, including a few stops along the way for the scientific experiments.

His cellphone rang and he pulled it out of his pocket. When the name "Captain America" flashed on the screen, he grinned and pressed it to his ear. "Hey, Tom. I was just thinking of you."

"Ren, I wish we could've caught up while you were here." Tom trained SEALs at Coronado.

The man was twelve years older than Ren. He'd already been working his way up in the Navy when he'd caught a teenage Ren trying to steal his car.

The memory made Ren smile. Tom was a regular Captain America. He was clean-cut and broad-shouldered. A man who lived and breathed his values, and always did the right thing. He regularly told Ren that it was an honor to serve his country.

He'd seen something in Ren. Something Ren hadn't seen. As a teenager, he'd believed he was only good enough to run with the other troublemaker kids he had grown up with. He'd been on the verge of turning from petty crime to much, much worse.

He blew out a breath. But Tom had changed everything. The man had challenged Ren to join the military. He'd told him to stop pretending to be a tough guy. That tough men and women wore uniforms.

And the toughest of the tough were the Navy SEALs. Ren had joined the Navy on a dare, and his life hadn't been the same since.

He'd found a purpose, a sense of belonging, and a family.

He smiled. Tom had become a mentor, best friend—hell, even a bit of a father or brother figure. Not that Tom would ever admit that.

Usually, when Ren was in town, they tried to connect, but they were both often busy. "Next time, Captain America, you can buy the beers. And grill me a decent steak."

"If you weren't married to the ocean, I'd see you more," Tom complained. "You're always on some adventure out at sea. We haven't seen enough of you."

Ren gripped the back of his neck. There was a reason for that.

And that reason was five foot six, with long, brown hair, freckles, and brilliant-blue eyes.

"The sea is a demanding lady."

Tom snorted. "I know. Halle misses you, too."

Ren's hand squeezed on the phone. *Halle.* His best friend's daughter. Tom had married his childhood sweetheart young, and they'd had Halle while they were in their early twenties. Then they'd divorced before Halle was ten.

She was now a beautiful twenty-three-year-old. She'd studied Marine biology over on the East Coast, and was now doing some post-graduate studies locally. Ren had avoided her the last few years.

There was no way he'd ever betray Tom's trust. And he'd already come very close to crossing that line.

He needed to get a handle on the fact the woman who dominated his dreams was his best friend's daughter.

"I can't thank you enough for arranging your ship to take this project," Tom said. "It's vital."

Tom had called in a favor. The Navy project needed a research vessel, and Ren happened to work on one. The Office of Naval Research usually utilized the Scripps Institute's ships, but they were currently all out at sea on other projects.

"You know I'm happy to pull strings for you," Ren said. "You still haven't told me what this project is, though."

"You'll find out soon enough."

At that moment, two nondescript, white vans pulled up at the dock. People started getting out. One guy was gawking at the ship—he was tall and lanky with wire-rimmed glasses perched on his nose. Stereotypical scientist.

Then Ren watched a woman round the vehicle and bend over a box of gear.

Ren arched a brow.

She had a spectacular ass. She was wearing navy-blue shorts that lovingly hugged her derrière. He couldn't see the rest of her, and he wondered if it was as good as the back view.

It had been a while since he'd felt the shimmer of desire for a woman. Hell, it had been a long time since he'd had sex.

Hard to have an active sex life when the only woman he pictured touching was off limits.

"I have another surprise for you."

Tom was still talking.

Ren dragged his gaze off the woman's ass. "Oh?"

"It's been killing me not to tell you."

The woman straightened and turned.

And every one of Ren's muscles locked.

It couldn't be.

Long, brown hair danced in the breeze. She smiled widely, then laughed at something one of her team members said. The breeze carried the sound toward him.

"Halle's on the team," Tom said. "She's their marine biologist."

Shit. Ren couldn't respond. His gaze was frozen on her.

The rest of Halle Bradshaw was as gorgeous as the back. Her T-shirt clung to slim arms and full breasts.

Now desire rocketed through Ren—hot and sharp.

Fucking hell.

"You get to spend the next week with my little girl, Ren. On that ship of yours, you won't be able to get away from her."

Ren's hand squeezed the phone so hard the plastic creaked. "Right."

Then Halle lifted her head and their gazes clashed.

HALLE BRADSHAW SMILED as she walked up the gang plank of the *Atalanta*.

The sun was shining, and the salty scent of the sea that she loved, filled her lungs. She was heading out to sea. Doing what she loved.

The ship was impressive. The hull was painted a crisp navy-blue, and the superstructure on top was a brilliant white. Right at the top of the *Atalanta* was the main mast topped with several large white balls she knew housed the radar and antennas.

She stepped onto the deck.

It was hard to pay much attention to the ship. She was also going to see Ren.

"Look at this ship." Sammy, a fellow scientist with a heavy Brooklyn accent stepped up beside her. "*Nice.*" Then she looked past Halle. "Something else is mighty fine, too."

Halle turned her head and saw Ren.

Lorenzo Santoro.

He was six feet of hard-packed muscle. His black hair was thick, with its usual, tousled look, and his skin tanned. The man loved being outdoors. He had a chiseled face, and deep, brown eyes that looked warm and velvety. The man was pure sin. Designed to make a woman's mind go foggy.

And imagine wicked things.

Just one look at him and her pulse went crazy. Like it always did when she saw him these days.

Not that she'd seen much of him lately. He'd been avoiding her very neatly for the last three years.

Once, he'd been a staple in her life, and then...

Well, then they'd shared the hottest, most life-altering kiss of her life on her 20th birthday.

Since then, Ren had gone AWOL. Always out on the ship, or off helping military buddies, or conveniently unavailable. The last time she'd seen him was about six months ago at her dad's place, when she'd turned up unexpectedly. Ren had said hello to her and left ten minutes later.

Her fingers curled into her palm, and she lifted her chin.

She'd given him time. She'd dedicated herself to her studies and college life. She'd tried not to think about him.

It hadn't really worked out as well as she'd hoped.

They were adults. They could work this out. She missed him.

She knew she might be young, but she knew all too well that life could be short. Losing her mom had painted that picture in the starkest possible way. She wanted Ren back in her life.

She pinned on a smile. "I know that something mighty fine."

Sammy blinked. "Really?"

"Really. He's my dad's best friend." Halle strode across the deck.

Ren stood watching her, looking wary.

God, butterflies took flight in her belly. Why did he have to look so good? "Ren," she said. "*Surprise.*"

"Halle." A small smile tipped his lips.

She threw her arms around him. Oh, it felt good to hug him.

His muscular arms closed around her. She closed her eyes and breathed him in. Ren always smelled like the ocean. "It's so good to see you."

He pulled back, his dark gaze meeting hers. Then he lifted a hand, like he was going to touch her face. But a second later, he let his hand drop to his side. "It's good to see you too, Ariel."

Her heart squeezed at the pet name. "I haven't watched *The Little Mermaid* for a really long time."

He grinned. "God, you loved that movie. Used to drive your dad crazy."

She hummed a few bars of "Under the Sea".

Ren snorted.

Oh, it felt good to talk with him. Joke with him. She'd missed that so much. "You know I prefer older movies now."

He shook his head. "Preferably black and white, and corny."

"Hey." She slapped his arm. "Don't pretend you don't love them as well."

She'd been so happy when she'd discovered their mutual love of old movies and TV shows.

He stepped back. "So, you're part of this Navy project?"

She nodded. "It's part of my master's project. I'm not working on the main project, but I'm assessing its impact on marine life."

He smiled at her again. It was sexy and panty-melting, and she pressed her thighs together.

"You and your dolphins."

"Not just dolphins," she said. "I love all marine life. Fish. Seals. Even sharks."

"No one likes sharks, Halle."

"Sure, they do. They're majestic creatures."

Ren shook his head.

"Halle?" Sammy stood there with a brow raised.

Behind her was the rest of the team.

"Ren, I'd like you to meet my team members," Halle said. "Everyone, this is Lorenzo Santoro."

Ren inclined his head. "I'm second in command of the *Atalanta*. If there is anything you need while you're aboard, I'm here to get it for you."

"This is Sammy Sorvino," Halle said.

Her dark-haired friend nodded. "A pleasure."

"And this is Fitz Armstrong."

"Hello," Fitz said, in his posh British accent. He gave his glasses a nudge and swallowed. "I'm warning you now, I suffer from terrible seasickness." He held up an arm, showing off several patches pressed to his skin. "These are supposed to help."

Sammy snorted. "I think you're only supposed to wear one, Fitz."

"I'm taking no chances."

Ren raised a brow. "It should be smooth sailing, Fitz, but if not, I have a few tricks to help you out. And seasickness usually only lasts the first twenty-fours hours, until you adjust."

Fitz's nose wrinkled.

"This is Ryan Hughes," Halle continued.

Ryan straightened, and gave Ren a nod. He had well-cut, blond hair and could be overconfident to the point of being a pain, but he was a good engineer.

Halle smiled. "And this is Professor Davis. He's in charge."

"Mark Davis. Thank you for having us, Mr. Santoro." The professor held out his hand. He was in his fifties, about five foot nine, with a slim build. He was always frowning, like there was a problem that needed solving. His hair was black, with gray at the temples. "We're excited to get to work on our testing."

Ren shook the man's hand. "Welcome aboard the *Atalanta*. It's a pleasure to have you with us. Please call me Ren. I'm here to make sure everything runs smoothly."

"And you know Halle." It was Ryan who spoke. He was frowning at Ren, and didn't look happy.

Halle hid her eye roll. Ryan had asked her out a few times, and she'd tried to tell him she wasn't interested, firmly but politely.

"We're family friends," Ren said.

"We need to get our gear aboard," Professor Davis said.

Ren nodded. "I'll have my team help you, and show you where you can store everything." He lifted a hand to wave at some crew members on the deck.

"There are a few things I want to bring on board myself," Ryan said. "I don't want anyone touching them but me." He straightened, his chest puffing up. "Our project is highly classified."

Ren stared at the young man like he was an insect. "Knock yourself out."

Halle coughed. "Ryan, Ren probably has higher clearance than you do."

"What?" Ryan looked startled.

"Ren was a Navy SEAL," she said.

"Really?" Sammy drawled.

Fitz blinked. "That's a very dangerous profession."

"I'm retired now," Ren said.

"And he's done other very badass stuff that's very, very classified," Halle continued.

"Halle," Ren said, before he looked at the others. "I'm just a sailor on a research vessel these days. Let's get you all settled. We'll get your gear aboard, then I'll hand out your cabin assignments."

"I'm keen to see the lab, as well," Professor Davis said.

"Sure thing. It's fully equipped."

As the *Atalanta* crew members arrived, Halle listened to Ren issuing orders. He just had an innate authority that told you he could handle any situation. She watched the way his muscular body moved. His polo shirt was fitted enough to cling to his muscular chest and biceps. Tingles traveled all over her.

"Girl, you've been holding out on me." Sammy murmured.

Halle wrinkled her nose. "He sees me as a little girl."

Sammy looked her up and down. "That would be impossible."

"He's my dad's best friend, Sammy."

"Oh." Sammy nodded sadly. "That puts you in the DNT zone." She slapped Halle's shoulder. "Do not touch. That sucks."

Halle usually liked Sammy's forthright nature, but now was not one of those times.

She dragged in a breath. She was here to work, not focus on the man she couldn't stop thinking about. Her work was important to her, and she wanted this project to be a success.

She had no idea what she wanted from Ren. *Liar*, a little voice whispered in her head.

Closing her eyes, she tried to settle herself. She would do her work, and spend some time with Ren. He was important to her.

And if he kissed her again, well, she wouldn't say no.

He couldn't avoid her when they were both on the same ship together.

CHAPTER TWO

Ren heaved a box, then carried it into the storage room on the main deck, and set it down. The team had a lot of gear.

He'd been trying to avoid Halle and doing anything to keep himself busy.

Halle was on his ship. His hands fisted.

Seeing her again had been like a punch to the gut. Young, gorgeous, a smile that lit up the room. She was so beautiful.

He never should have kissed her. It had been during her 20th birthday party. He'd gone to get a beer from the kitchen, and she'd been there in a pretty, blue dress. Just the two of them. They'd talked, laughed, and it had just happened.

And it had been fucking amazing.

"She's your best friend's daughter, asshole," he muttered.

Not to mention he'd seen shit, done shit. Shit she would never understand. Things he never wanted her to know. Old memories cluttered in his head, making his heart squeeze. They'd faded over time, but they never went away—a woman's scream, a girl's broken sobbing, a man's roar of anguish.

Ren shook his head. He didn't deserve to touch someone as fresh and gorgeous and good as Halle. She had her whole life ahead of her, and she deserved someone without his kind of baggage.

Not to mention, Tom would kill him.

"Ren, where do you want these?" A crew member, Sean, appeared, with a heavy-duty crate in his hands.

Ren jerked his head. "Over there." Turning, he scanned the deck and saw Captain Shroff approaching from the upper deck.

Shroff was an older man, with a weathered face, and a long, black beard speckled with gray. He wore a white polo shirt with the ship's logo on it. "Ren."

"Jay." He had an excellent working relationship with the older man. Jay Shroff was a hell of a captain, and knew everything about ships, sailing, and the sea.

"Everything stowed?"

"Almost. And I've assigned the scientists their cabins." He'd done a last-minute switch to ensure that Halle was close to his stateroom. Just so he could keep an eye on her.

That was the *only* reason.

"Excellent." The captain nodded. "We have a briefing with the research team in the mess."

Ren nodded and followed the other man up the stairs. The next level of the ship held the dining room, galley, a small lounge and some cabins. He followed Jay into the mess. It was spacious, with a wall of windows framing the water, and several wooden tables that were bolted to the floor. From the sounds coming from the adjoining galley, he knew their often- unpredictable Russian chef was busy getting all the supplies put away. Ren made a mental note to talk with Petrov and soothe any ruffled feathers over the supplies.

But none of that mattered right now because Ren's gaze went straight to Halle. She was sitting with the rest of her team at one of the tables.

When she saw him, she smiled.

And he felt a damn stutter in his chest.

Ren cleared his throat. "Everyone, I'd like to introduce our captain. Captain Shroff, this is the research team."

Professor Davis rose and stepped forward. "I can't tell you how excited we all are for this trip."

The captain nodded and shook the man's hand. "Welcome aboard the *Atalanta*, the finest research vessel on the seas. We'll do everything we can to make this a productive trip for you."

The professor nodded. "Thank you."

"Now, in order to make that happen, we need you to tell us more about your project, Professor." Ren hitched a hip against one of the tables. "You're aware that both the captain and I have security clearance."

The man nodded. "Of course. Our project code name is Deep Water. We're testing a next-generation UUV."

Ren raised a brow. An unmanned underwater vehicle, or underwater drone. The *Atalanta* had several submersibles and ROVs aboard—all state-of-the-art. But some of the remote operated vehicles were on tethers, or couldn't go very far from the ship before they needed re-charging.

But he knew that wasn't what this team was testing. He knew the Navy had been experimenting with UUVs that could go longer distances, and operate for long periods of time.

"You're talking about something like DARPA's manta ray drone?" he asked.

"Similar," the professor replied. "The Defense Advanced Research Projects Agency drone project runs alongside ours. The manta ray is a large UUV, one they want to make capable of carrying a payload. Our project has the potential to align with that one in the future."

"And you may have heard of the GhostSwimmer." Ryan pulled a face. "Hotshots out of MIT are working with the Navy on that one. Looks like a shark, and moves like one too. They're trying to mimic the dynamic movements of a fish."

Ren frowned. "So how is your drone different?"

"It's not the actual UUV we're testing," the professor said. "Our design is small and quite simple."

"We're testing a new power method," Sammy said.

Professor Davis nodded. "The problem with most UUVs has always been fuel. Whatever they're fueled by can't last long enough. They either need to return to a base, or be re-fueled or re-charged some way before they can even get very far."

"That's where our drone's different." Fitz leaned forward, brushing his sandy hair off his pale face. He was looking a little queasy. "We're here to test an experimental hydrogen fuel cell."

Ren's eyebrows went up. "I thought hydrogen fuel cells weren't really viable."

"They haven't been for cars," Professor Davis said. "They aren't as clean or efficient as electric options, and the infrastructure isn't there."

"But," Sammy said. "Hydrogen fuel cells can go farther and refuel much faster."

"And our new fuel cell is smaller than anything created before," Professor Davis said proudly, "and if our tests go well, we can confirm we could run a UUV for not weeks or months, but *years*."

Hell. "A lot of people would be interested in that," Ren said. Including a lot of unfriendly governments and terrorist groups.

"Yes, that's why our project is highly classified," the professor continued. "Once our UUV passes testing, it will change the landscape of underwater drones."

"Then we need your test plan, so we can ensure you achieve everything you need on this trip," Captain Shroff said.

"I'll also be running several tests, and have sensors on the UUV," Halle said. "To assess its sound levels and impact on the marine wildlife."

The captain nodded. "We want this to be a smooth trip to Hawaii for all of us."

Fitz raised a hand. "Smooth would be good. Really good."

Sammy elbowed the man. "Sweetie, you need to toughen up."

"Easy for you to say, since you're actually tough, and I'm..." He waved at his slim build.

Halle rose. "Now that everything's aboard, we're planning to celebrate the beginning of our trip. We're going to a local bar here at the docks. The Ketch Bar and Taps. I hear it has good beer. All the *Atalanta* crew are invited."

Ren felt her gaze shift to him. Shit, going to drink with Halle wasn't a good idea. He gave a brief nod. "If I have time, I'll stop in."

He watched her face dim.

He looked at the crew seated at the nearby tables. "If you're not on shift, you're welcome to go."

As everyone rose and started to leave the mess, Halle came over and grabbed his arm. "Ren, please come. I haven't seen you in forever."

"Halle, I have a lot to do—"

"Please." Her eyes were a shimmering blue.

He was so weak. "I'll come."

The smile that broke out on her face was blinding. "I'm glad."

He wanted to stay right there, close to her. He wanted to catch up, hear her laugh. He made himself step back. "Then I'll see you later."

Ren strode out of the mess, then paused on the stairs. "You're an idiot, Santoro."

He cared for Halle, and he'd promised Tom he'd take care of her.

That meant not touching her. And definitely not kissing her.

HALLE TOOK another small sip of her one glass of wine. She scanned the bar. The Ketch Bar and Taps had a modern tavern vibe, with lots of wood and metal. It had an amazing back deck overlooking all the boats in the marina.

There was no sign of Ren.

She tried to hide her disappointment. There were plenty of other crew members from the *Atalanta* who'd joined them at the bar for a while.

He wasn't coming.

She was wearing her favorite jeans that did great things for her ass, and a fitted blue shirt that matched her eyes. She'd spent way too long on her hair, which was loose in gentle waves. She'd kept her makeup natural, because she hated too much makeup, and usually didn't wear much.

Around her, the others were chatting, talking with the ship's crew, enjoying their drinks.

She took another sip of her white wine.

There was something between her and Ren.

Ever since that kiss, she'd known it.

And she knew *him*. He was an honorable man, who could be funny and charming. She knew he'd done tough missions in the military. Over the years, she'd seen him harden—the lines bracketing his mouth had deepened, the look in his eyes had darkened, he laughed less.

She'd hoped when he'd left the military, she'd see more of him. But since he'd gotten the job on the *Atalanta,* she'd rarely seen him.

Was she kidding herself? She was twenty-three years old. She was smart, and hard-working, but she didn't have his experience. She knew he used to be quite the ladies' man—her father had mentioned it.

She could easily see why any woman would take one look at Ren Santoro and be attracted. The hard, muscular body, the handsome face, the charming grin.

She took a larger sip of wine.

She'd gone to college and tried to move on. Hell, when a man kisses you, then runs away to sea to avoid you, it's not great for the confidence.

Had he hated kissing her that much?

She spun the stem of her glass in her hand. She'd dated other guys, but never let it go very far. Because whenever she thought of being with a man, she thought of Ren.

"You look like someone stole your favorite toy." Sammy appeared, sipping a large cocktail with a pink umbrella in it.

"I was hoping Ren would come. He said he would. I should've known he'd avoid me." Halle sipped her wine again, but this mouthful tasted like vinegar. "He's good at it."

"Girl, I get the attraction to the older, sexy man. You sure he's the one you want?"

"It's not just his looks, Sammy. He's a great guy. He's a hero. He had this entire military career he can't talk about. He served his country." She sighed. "He loves old sci-fi TV shows like me. We used to watch them together when I was younger. We're both addicted to cotton candy. He sends me bags of it on my birthday." She pressed a hand to her chest. "Maybe you're right. I'm imagining he likes me the way I like him. I mean, he could have anyone."

Sammy was staring at her.

"What?"

"He sends you cotton candy?"

"Yes."

"Halle, he could have anyone. The guy is gorgeous. And even if he isn't an asshole, which it sounds like he isn't, you're the full package. Smart, pretty, kind. Nice."

Halle wrinkled her nose. "No one wants to be called nice. We all know that's code for boring."

"You're not boring, but you, Ms. Bradshaw, are one of those positive people who looks on the bright side all the time. Even when it's pouring rain, and the boat is sinking."

Halle rolled her eyes. "Let's not talk about sinking boats before we set sail, on a boat, to Hawaii. And I'm only positive in contrast to you, who loves her mean, tough Brooklyn vibe."

Sammy's lips twitched. "Trust me. Just spend some time around him and be yourself. He'll cave." Her friend took another sip of her cocktail. "Ryan won't be happy."

"I'm not interested in Ryan. He's asked me out, and I turned him down. He's..."

"A little cocksure and overconfident."

"He just needs to grow up a bit."

"Especially for the girl with eyes only for the older hottie."

The older hottie who clearly wasn't going to show

tonight. She sighed. "I'm going out the back to get some air."

Sammy took Halle's wine glass and nodded. "Chin up."

Halle stepped out onto the back deck. Now that night had fallen, it was cool outside, so there weren't too many people sitting at the tables. Spring was coming, but the air was still brisk. She pulled on her jacket.

She saw a couple at one table, hands entwined, smiling at each other.

Her chest tightened, and she kept walking. She stepped off the deck, listening to the lap of water on the moored boats. There was a small side alley, no doubt to give access to people who owned the boats. She spotted a few more tables with umbrellas, but no one was sitting at them.

Her thoughts were all tangled up on Ren.

She walked past the tables. The alley was blissfully quiet.

You're in charge of your feelings, Halle. You need to stop obsessing over the man.

Suddenly, tires squealed on pavement. She looked up and saw a black van back into the alley, fast.

What the hell?

The vehicle screeched to a halt in front of her, and the side door was flung open. Two men in black ski masks leaped out.

Halle stumbled back.

One man lunged forward and grabbed her.

"Hey!" Adrenaline hit her system. "Let me go!"

This couldn't be happening.

She fought, twisting her body, and trying to wrench her arm free. She was the daughter of a Navy SEAL, after all. Her father had taught her some self-defense moves. She rammed an elbow back into the man's stomach and heard him grunt.

She yanked her arm down and out, managing to break his hold. But a second later, the other guy was on her.

He wrapped his arms around her from behind and dragged her toward the van.

Halle opened her mouth and screamed.

CHAPTER THREE

Ren pushed open the front door to the Ketch Bar.

He shouldn't be here. He knew he needed to limit his exposure to Halle.

He spotted the group sitting by the bar, but didn't see her. He and his crew mates came to the Ketch pretty regularly. He liked the craft beer. He spotted Wonder Boy—Ryan—laughing, his face flushed. He looked like he'd had one drink too many.

Ren knew his type. Always needing to prove who was bigger, tougher, and smarter.

Ren reached the bar and ordered a blonde ale.

"You made it, Hottie Ren." The dark-haired woman from the research team leaned against the bar. "Halle will be happy."

"Sammy, right?"

"Right."

Ren lifted his beer and scanned the bar again. Still no pretty brunette. "Where is Halle?"

"She stepped out the back for some air. I think she

was trying to choke back her disappointment because she thought you weren't coming."

His chest tightened.

Sammy frowned and glanced at her watch. "She's been gone a while."

Instantly, Ren felt it. That tickle between his shoulder blades. His instincts were well-developed after being a SEAL, then in Ghost Ops. He'd had years to refine them. They'd saved his life, and the lives of his buddies, too many times to count.

He set his beer down. "I'll check on her."

He pushed through the crowd and reached the doors to the back deck. Boats bobbed in the marina, and off to the right, he saw the lights of the city. There were only a few people sitting on the deck—where he and the crew liked to sit in the summer—but none of them were Halle.

He moved toward the railing. Still no Halle.

A woman screamed.

He broke into a run. He pressed a hand to the wooden railing and vaulted over it. As he landed, he saw Halle in the side alley, struggling with two masked men. There was a van, with its door open, idling beside them.

Rage hit him.

Halle was in danger.

He didn't make a sound. He just charged forward and into the fight.

Protect Halle. That was the only thing that reverberated in his head.

He grabbed the first man, and spun him around violently.

"What the—?"

Before the guy could finish, Ren jabbed the side of his flat palm to the man's neck.

The guy gagged and doubled over. Ren hooked a foot around the man's leg and sent him crashing to the pavement.

He spun, advancing on the other man who was holding Halle.

Her blue eyes were wide, terrified. They locked on him.

He saw her mouth his name.

"You shouldn't have touched her." Ren's voice was low and deadly.

The man tightened his hold on her. "Back off, asshole."

Ren kept his arms relaxed at his side. "Let her go, and I won't break your jaw."

Through the ski mask, the man's eyes widened.

Ren was done. The fucker had his hands on Halle.

Ren attacked. He dodged around Halle and rammed a punch into the man's side. The guy yelped, released Halle, and shoved her. She flew forward and fell on her hands and knees.

Mouth flattening, Ren hammered another punch into the man's face. With a roar, the man swung an arm at Ren. He caught it and used it to swing the asshole around. He rammed a knee into the attacker's gut.

The guy tried to kick Ren, but he deflected, and aimed another hard punch to the man's face. He heard a crack.

The man howled and clutched his jaw.

"I warned you," Ren said.

Ignoring the two men now groaning on the ground, he spun to Halle. "Are you okay?"

She was on her knees, hair disheveled and her eyes wet, but she lifted her chin. "I'm fine."

She had a streak of stubborn in her, that was for sure. Since she'd lost her mom, she hated crying.

Then her eyes went wide as she looked over his shoulder. "Ren, watch out!"

Moving on instinct, he dodged to the side.

A knife rushed past him.

Whirling, he grabbed the man's arm and twisted. The knife dropped to the ground.

Then Ren swung the asshole, slamming him into the side of the van.

The second man staggered up, looking dazed.

The two of them glanced at Halle, but Ren stepped in front of her. He raised his fists. "You want more, I'll give you more. You should never have touched her."

"Fuck this," one muttered. He dived into the back of the van. The second guy hesitated, then followed him.

Ren flexed his hand. He watched the door slam shut and the van sped down the alley. He wanted to go after them. He'd sell what was left of his soul to go after them.

The van screeched out on the road and sped away.

But Halle needed him.

He turned. He had to make sure she was okay, had to keep her safe.

"Halle?" He dropped to one knee beside her.

"Ren." There was a tremor in her voice. Then she

threw herself at him, colliding with his chest. He hugged her hard.

"You're okay?" He stroked a hand gently down her back.

"I will be." Her voice was shaky. "*God.*"

"Did you know them?"

"No." She shook her head. "They just pulled up and tried to grab me." She shivered.

He kept stroking her back. "You're safe now." *Fuck.* If he'd been just a few minutes later...

He could have lost her.

He tightened his hold, and she turned her face into his neck.

THE FEAR and adrenaline were fading.

She was in Ren's arms.

Halle clung to him, breathing in the crisp scent of his cologne. She was safe. She dragged in a deep breath. She was with Ren.

He'd stormed in to save her.

Not like a hero. No, the look on his face had been too deadly. He'd looked like a dark angel.

"Halle." He cupped her face. His concerned brown gaze ran over her.

"I'm all right." She shifted, then winced as her knees stung.

He looked down. "Your jeans are torn. You're bleeding." His tone was fierce. Then he lifted one of her hands. They were scraped, as well. "These need to be cleaned."

"What happened?" someone yelled from the deck.

"Halle, God." Sammy raced down the steps toward them. "Are you all right?"

"Yes." Halle looked up and saw a small crowd gathered on the deck. She spotted her colleagues and several *Atalanta* crew, all frowning.

A Ketch staff member stood by the rail. "I've called the police. Is anyone hurt?"

"I'm fine," Halle said. "I just scraped my hands and knees."

"Two men tried to grab her," Ren said.

"Someone tried to snatch you?" Sammy's face was fierce. "Those fuckers."

Halle's chest felt tight. "I don't want any drama. I'm safe. That's the important thing."

Ren was frowning at her. "You need to talk to the cops."

"Do I have to?" All she wanted was to wash her hands, put her pajamas on, and curl up in bed. "We'll be gone tomorrow. I don't want to cause a fuss."

"You will be far from those assholes tomorrow, and they won't get near you again." He paused. "But they could try to snatch some other woman."

She sucked in a sharp breath. She hadn't thought of that. "Oh, no." She couldn't let that happen.

Ren took her hand and squeezed gently. "I'll be with you the entire time." Then his face hardened, and he stared down the alley. He jerked his head at Professor Davis.

The man hurried over, brow creased. "Halle? Are you sure you don't need medical attention?"

"No, Professor. It's just a few scrapes."

"Professor," Ren lowered his voice. "Any chance these people trying to snatch Halle are related to the project?"

Professor Davis's eyes widened. "I...I don't think so."

Halle felt her stomach do a sickening swirl. "Ren, I'm the team marine biologist. I know next to nothing about the workings of the fuel cell."

Ren's frown deepened. "You're sure? You possibly have access to some of the data."

She shrugged a shoulder. "It would make much more sense to grab one of the others. They're the engineers."

Professor Davis nodded. "She's right."

Just then, a San Diego squad car pulled in.

"All right," Ren said. "Halle, you need to give your statement to the officers."

She nodded.

Soon, she found herself sitting at a table on the deck with two officers and Ren. She tugged at the sleeves of her shirt.

The older cop, Officer Bates, pulled out a notepad and nodded. "Start at the beginning, Ms. Bradshaw."

Halle told them everything that had happened since she'd stepped outside.

"So you didn't get a good look at them?" the younger female cop, Officer Ramirez, asked.

"No, sorry. They were both wearing ski masks."

"One was six feet tall," Ren said. "My height, slightly smaller build. The other guy was stockier, a few inches shorter, and had brown eyes. Both were white. I saw the skin on their forearms."

Halle blinked. He'd noticed all that?

The officers scribbled notes.

"Both had worn-in boots, and some training. They knew what they were doing."

"Military?" Officer Bates asked.

"Possibly," Ren said. "The van was black, a Ford, no plates."

Officer Ramirez glanced at her partner, then back at Ren and Halle. "We'll pass along this information and see if we can track down the van."

"The reality is," Officer Bates said, "that it's not uncommon for people to get snatched off the streets. We aren't far from the border with Mexico. Several gangs are involved in human trafficking, and they target pretty, young women."

"Their favorite prey are women who were alone," Officer Ramirez added. "The perfect target.

God. Halle pressed her palm to her belly. She felt sick.

The officers rose.

"If you think of anything else, give us a call," Officer Bates said.

"Thank you." Ren slid an arm around Halle's shoulders. "We appreciate your time." He waited for them to leave. "You okay?"

"Yes. No." She sighed. "Maybe."

He squeezed her closer. "You'll be fine. You have that tough Bradshaw core, but if you need to cry or yell, I'm here."

She smiled. "I'm not going to cry or yell." She touched his shoulder, then as her hand stung, she winced.

He took her wrist and studied her palm. His jaw tightened. "These need cleaning. Let's get you back to the ship."

It felt nice to let him look after her. "Thanks, Ren."

REN HELPED HALLE out of the Uber.

She smiled her thanks. The hull of the *Atalanta* rose up above them. Suddenly, Ren scooped her up into his arms.

Oh. She felt like her insides turned to jello. She cleared her throat. "I can walk."

"I don't care." He carried her all the way to the ship, and up the gang plank.

She liked it. Being held in his arms. She slid her arm across his broad shoulders. He carried her so easily.

Once aboard, he headed up the next set of stairs and straight to his cabin. She realized his was just a few doors down from her own.

When he pushed open the door, she saw his was a lot more spacious than hers.

"This is nice."

"Perks of being one of the bosses. We get a stateroom." He set her down on the double bed. "Don't move."

He ducked into the adjoining bathroom, and she heard cabinets opening. She glanced around. The cabin was simple, with a TV built into a cabinet, a desk, and a small couch. She spotted a few framed photos on the desk and arched her neck to see. One was of two older women with dark hair. She guessed it was his mom and *abuela.* Another was with a group of men she guessed were military friends. One was of him and her dad. Then she saw the last one.

It was a photo of her. From her 20th birthday.

Her chest tightened.

He returned with a first aid kit. "I'll start with your scraped knee." Then he frowned at her. "You'll have to take your jeans off."

Her pulse went crazy. "Right."

He turned.

She stared at his back for a second, trying not to think about getting undressed with Ren in the room. And what that did to her pulse. She quickly toed her shoes off, then shimmied the denim off her legs, and gave the hem of her shirt a tug. It was long enough to cover her panties, at least.

"All done."

He turned and froze for a second. His gaze ran down her legs, and she felt it like he'd touched her.

Then he knelt in front of her.

Everything inside her went crazy. Ren, the man she'd dreamed about, was kneeling in front of her, right by her bare legs. She felt tingles start up in her belly and arrow between her legs.

Halle sucked in a breath, trying to get a handle on her desire.

But Ren was all business. He pulled open the red kit, opened some packets, and then started cleaning her scratched knees.

She hissed at the sting.

"Sorry."

"It's fine. I'm just a wimp."

"Hardly, Ariel. You did well fighting those guys off."

"I can't be Tom Bradshaw's daughter and not know some self-defense."

"Right." A muscle ticked in Ren's jaw.

Halle glanced away. Reminding him who her father was probably wasn't a great idea.

"Hands next," he ordered.

She held them out, watching as his dark head bent over her hands. His hair was pitch black, and thick. She itched to run her fingers through it.

"I missed you," she said quietly.

He looked up.

"You stopped coming around."

He was quiet for a moment. "I know. I was busy."

"That wasn't it." She touched his shoulder, feeling the warm muscle beneath the soft cotton. "Don't brush it aside, Ren. You've been ignoring me since we kissed."

Ren snapped the first aid kit shut and stood. "That kiss shouldn't have happened, Halle."

She made an annoyed sound and stood. "We were two consenting adults. And it was a good kiss. A really good kiss."

"Halle..."

"I won't let you ignore it. I still think about it."

"It can't happen," he gritted out.

She stood, feeling the intensity swirling in the air between them. "You felt it, just like I did. That glimmer of something important."

He shook his head.

God, was she just a young woman spinning a fantasy about the handsome, older guy? Was she only seeing what she wanted to believe? She touched a hand to his chest and felt his heart beating hard.

Her own heart leaped. He wasn't immune to her. "You feel it, too."

"No," he said.

"Don't lie to me, Ren."

He gripped her wrist. "It can't happen."

"Why?"

"So many reasons. You're too young, I'm too old."

She made a scoffing sound. "That's really lame."

"You have your life ahead of you."

"You do too, Ren. Your life outside the military."

"No, I'm... I've seen too much, Halle. Things you'd never understand." He let her go and held up his palm. "These hands should never touch you."

She reached out and gripped his wrist. She pulled his hand flat to her chest. "I want them to. Tell me that you don't feel it, and I'll walk away."

A muscle ticked in his jaw, and he looked away.

She should feel like she'd won. Without words, he was admitting that he wanted her.

"There's another reason," he said. "I won't betray your father. He's the best man I know." A grimace crossed Ren's face, then he made himself step back. His face was set in harsh lines. "I have things to see to on the ship. You can see yourself out."

Then he was gone.

Halle sat there for a second, staring at the empty doorway. Then her shoulders sagged.

Okay, that hadn't exactly gone well.

But she wasn't giving up. Ren was wrong. He felt something, and so did she.

He was worth fighting for.

CHAPTER FOUR

Ren stood on the main deck, staring out at the horizon.

They were underway.

He listened to the familiar rumble of the ship's engines. It was still early, the sun barely over the horizon, but they'd already left the California coast far behind.

Had Halle slept all right? Had she had any nightmares? He shoved his hands in his pockets. He knew all about nightmares. The bad dreams that clawed you awake, soaking your sheets with sweat.

He gripped the railing, hands curling tight.

What if he hadn't gone to the bar last night? His gut tightened. He almost hadn't because he'd been determined to avoid her.

To avoid the temptation.

She was safe. That was the important thing.

And he'd keep her that way during this trip.

Plus, he'd keep his hands off her.

You felt it. Just like me. The glimmer of something important.

He muttered a curse, then heard voices. Ren turned and spotted some of his crew on the deck, going about their duties.

Then, some of the scientists began to appear, all looking a little sleepy, or hungover. Ryan was yawning as he started opening some of their boxes.

"Good morning."

When Ren heard Halle's voice behind him, he turned.

She smiled at him, but he noted the dark smudges under her eyes. She was holding two mugs of coffee, steam curling off the top.

"For you." She handed him one. "Cream and three sugars."

Just how he liked it. His Ghost Ops buddies had liked to rib him to no end because he liked sweet coffee.

"Thanks." He took a mug. "You didn't sleep well."

She shrugged a slim shoulder. "First night somewhere new." She blew out a breath. "And a few bad moments, but I know I'm safe out here." She sipped her coffee and looked at the ocean. "No one can get me aboard a ship."

Something about those guys trying to grab her still nagged him. Traffickers tended to target vulnerable women who wouldn't be missed. Something didn't add up.

"You're sure you didn't recognize those men?"

She turned to him. "No."

"Any other people who might do something like this?"

"Ren, are you asking if I have enemies?" She laughed. "I'm a marine biologist."

"Angry ex?"

"No. There's no angry ex."

He already hated any man she'd dated. He took a drink of his coffee to wash down the bad taste in his mouth. "We'd better get to work."

As she headed down the steps, the rest of her team called out hellos and Halle waved at them. Ren's gaze drifted down her legs. Why did she have to wear shorts so short?

She glanced back, and caught him looking. She shot him a smile.

Ren pressed his lips together. She joined the others, and he watched them start prepping their computers and gear. Then, they gathered around a large box made of tough, black metal. The professor tapped a code into the electronic lock and it opened.

Ren walked closer and got his first look at the UUV.

It wasn't anything fancy. It was torpedo-shaped, with two fins off the side, and made of a dark-gray metal.

"That it?" Jack, one of Ren's security guys asked.

"Yeah. If this new fuel cell technology works, the Navy will be giddy." Ren frowned. "And if others get wind of it, they'll want it, too."

Jack, a former Marine, nodded. "We'd better go over our security plan. Although no one can sneak up on us easily out here."

Ren sipped his coffee without replying. He was a SEAL, and they'd infiltrated plenty of ships. And in Ghost Ops, they'd snuck into some damn-near impossible places. He knew it was possible.

The morning ticked away. Ren oversaw the crew and their regular duties. Soon, the sun was high overhead. The research team was still hard at work, setting up their lab.

Ren kept an eye on them, hoping to catch glimpses of Halle. She looked focused and competent as she went about her work. It was clear that she was good at her job.

He made himself turn away. He had his own job to do.

A few hours later, the *Atalanta* slowed to a stop.

Captain Shroff appeared. "Time for the first UUV test."

They all moved to the back deck of the ship. Some of the crew members hooked the UUV drone to the small crane at the stern. Moments later, the crane activated, and lifted the drone over the water.

Halle stood nearby, holding a heavy-duty tablet in her hands. She was frowning at the screen.

Ren headed in her direction. "Okay?"

She gave him an absent-minded nod. "Yes. There are lots of sensors on the UUV for my research. Noise levels, water temperature. I'm just getting them all calibrated for the first test."

There was a splash as the UUV lowered into the water.

The team moved around excitedly. Ryan had a large

laptop resting on top of some crates. "All systems are in the green. Ready to launch."

"Launch," the professor said.

Ryan touched some buttons, and the UUV powered up. A second later, it sliced through the water. The rest of the team huddled around the laptop.

"Halle, is your data coming through?" Sammy asked.

"Yes." Halle gave a thumbs up.

"Fitz?" Sammy said. "How's your data looking?"

Fitz, who looked a pale shade of green, nodded. "Fine, I think... *God.*" The scientist spun, slapped a hand to his mouth, then ran across the deck. He hit the railing, leaned over, and barfed.

Ren winced. He guessed the patches weren't working. He needed to make sure poor Fitz stayed hydrated until the seasickness passed.

The team all started talking about things that Ren didn't understand. He shook his head. They were lost in their work.

He leaned against the railing. The UUV was out of sight now, and he only had eyes for Halle. She was absorbed by whatever was on her tablet. So damn smart. He'd always known that, but it was different to see it in action.

The team continued working, and it wasn't too long before the drone came back into view, stopping back at the side of the ship.

Ryan grinned. "Everything functioned as planned. Fuel cell is operating at optimal levels."

The team cheered.

Test one was complete.

HALLE HUNCHED OVER HER LAPTOP. She was in the computer lab, and it was late. She was going over her data.

She tapped the keyboard, staring up at the screens attached to the wall. She had to admit, the *Atalanta* was amazing. The computer lab, and attached main lab for testing, had everything a scientist could want.

The rest of her team had left for dinner a while ago, and Halle's empty stomach grumbled, reminding her that she should have gone, too. She reached for her half-eaten bag of chips.

"Working late?"

She looked up and saw Ren leaning in the doorway.

Her heart did a little stutter. His dark-blue polo shirt was stretched tight over his muscular chest and arms. Did he know how good that looked?

She'd been so aware of him today as she'd been working. Even when she'd been busy with the work she loved, she'd known exactly where he was. Usually standing on deck, unfazed by the pitch and roll of the ship.

"The sensors on the UUV collect data for me," she told him. "I'm just running some analyses on today's results."

"You missed dinner."

She smiled. "I got caught up with the sound information. I have a bit of a habit of doing that."

"You shouldn't miss a meal." He walked forward, and

set a mug and something wrapped in foil on the bench beside her.

She lifted the mug and smelled. "Hot chocolate."

"I know you like it."

"I do. Thanks." She took a sip and opened the foil.

"It's just a chicken salad sandwich," he said. "Nothing fancy."

"It's perfect." She lifted her arms and stretched out her stiff neck and shoulders. Then she took a big bite of the sandwich, chewed, and swallowed. "I think I need some fresh air."

Ren hesitated. "Come on. I know a spot."

Holding onto her mug, she stepped out of the lab, and Ren took her other hand. She bit her lip and curled her fingers with his.

He led her along the main deck, all the way to the front of the ship. She could see the water sloshing below as the *Atalanta* cut through the waves. He moved over to a large metal box and opened it, pulling out some blankets.

"You've done this before."

"The bow of the ship is one of the places I come to be alone." He wrapped a blanket around her shoulders, and she gripped it. "It can be hard to find solitude on a ship full of people sometimes."

"Look at the stars." She cradled her mug and looked up at the beautiful night sky. The Milky Way stretched overhead, sprinkled with stars. "You don't see stars like this in the city."

"One of the perks of living on a ship. Sunrise and

sunset over the ocean, the stars every night." He leaned back against the railing. "It's pretty amazing."

She eyed him. "You needed this. Being out here. The solitude." He turned to look at her. "After the military."

His face turned serious. "Ghost Ops was tough. When I came home..."

She reached out and touched his hand. "You can tell me, Ren."

His gaze bored into hers.

She wondered if he'd talked to anyone. She knew he caught up with her father frequently for beers and dinners. But something told her Ren kept what bothered him bottled up.

"Tell me," she murmured.

"I lost friends, good men." He shook his head. "Recently, I stayed with my friend Shep. He blamed himself when four of our guys got taken in an ambush." He blew out a breath. "We only got one out alive."

Her chest squeezed. "I'm so sorry, Ren."

"For me it wasn't just one thing. It was a slow trickle. Like a drip of all the terrible stuff that I saw. Terrible things. I spent some time working undercover." He shook his head. "I don't regret any of it. Everything I did was to protect my country." His gaze ran over her face. "Protect the innocent people who I never want to see those horrors. I knew it was time to get out. And at first it was hard. I think being on the *Atalanta* helped me smooth out some of my messed-up kinks. But they aren't all gone. They'll never be gone."

Halle gripped her blanket harder. "You're trying to

tell me that you're the older, experienced man, and I could never understand what you went through."

His mouth flattened. "Halle. You're—" he blew out a breath "—young, fresh, good. You have your life ahead of you. There's no way any asshole with baggage like mine should tarnish that."

She swiveled. "All I heard was young and naïve, and to run along and be a good girl."

"Halle—"

"No, Ren. Don't. I'm good at my work. I've been lucky to have a good father, but I went through a lot when I was growing up. Dad was away. All the time. I was incredibly close to my mom." Halle smiled, but it was tinged with sadness. She understood, just like Ren did, that grief never, ever went away. The dull throb of something missing. It wasn't always as keen these days, although it could attack hard some days when she least expected it. "Mom was awesome. She loved the ocean. Part of the reason I studied marine biology was because of her. I lost her, right when I was becoming a woman." She stared blindly at the dark sea. "So, I may not know combat, but I understand loss and hardship, Ren."

"I know, Ariel." He wrapped an arm around her. "I'm sorry you lost her."

The nickname warmed her again. "I was in the car with her. When we had the car accident."

"I know."

She closed her eyes. The warmth in his voice was getting to her. Right then and there, it felt like it was just the two of them in the entire world.

"Mom swerved to miss a dog, and then we hit another car. It pushed us into an intersection—"

Her voice cracked. The memories hit her like bullets, peppering hard—the sounds, the blows, the screams, the crunch of metal and breaking glass.

Ren's arm tightened on her, and he took her hand.

"She was bleeding," Halle whispered. "I was trapped, and freaked out, but I was mostly okay."

"You broke your leg. And two ribs."

She wasn't surprised he knew. "But I lived. I was trying to fight off an asthma attack, and I knew Mom was hurt bad." Her throat thickened. "She kept trying to reassure me. I held her hand." She met his warm brown gaze. "I held her hand as she died. Watched when she took her last breath."

"*Baby.*"

"It took them over an hour to get us out of the car."

And she'd sat there the whole time holding her mom's cooling fingers.

"Halle." He pulled her into his arms, and shuffled them a few steps. He sat down on a built-in bench and pulled her onto his lap. He was warm and strong, and she held on tight.

"I couldn't work out how she could just be gone," Halle murmured. "She'd made me breakfast that morning. She'd joked with me about this boy I liked at school. And then by that afternoon, she was gone."

"I'm sorry, baby." He rocked her.

"Dad came home from wherever he was." She touched Ren's face. "And someone special sent me an entire box of cotton candy." She stroked his stubble.

"Mom is why I try to do everything that matters, and give it one hundred percent. I don't want any regrets. If something feels right, and important, I've got to take the chance."

He stared into her gaze, emotions flickering through his eyes.

Then Halle leaned forward and touched her lips to his.

CHAPTER FIVE

H*alle.*

Hell, Halle was in his arms.

Ren's arms clenched on her, and he fought for control. Her sweet lips moved over his, giving him the briefest taste of her. His gut clenched.

Then she pulled back, and her blue eyes met his. "*Please.*"

Something inside him snapped.

He yanked her closer and kissed her.

He plundered her mouth, biting her lower lip before sliding his tongue into the sweetness of her mouth. Her lips were soft, warm, and perfect.

He'd kissed a lot of women in his life, but knowing he was kissing Halle right now nearly sent him over the edge.

She let out a husky moan, then shifted, straddling his hips and wrapping her arms around his shoulders. He cupped her ass with one hand, and slid the other into her hair. He tilted her head, taking the kiss deeper. She whimpered, her curvy body rubbing against him.

"You taste like sin," he growled. "Sweet, sweet sin."

"Please, Ren," she breathed against his mouth. "Keep kissing me."

"You want this sexy mouth kissed?" He fisted her hair tighter. "God, you tempt me. And every time I see these damn freckles..." He whispered his lips over the bridge of her nose.

"I should use more sunscreen."

"I love them." He took her mouth again. She moaned, her tongue stroking his. Her thighs hugged his waist, and she worked herself against him. Rubbing her sweet pussy against where he was hard as steel.

Having her this close set his blood on fire.

He kept kissing her, then she sucked on his tongue. *Fuck.* His cock was so hard it hurt.

He slid a hand up her body, and cupped her breast. The sexy, little sound she made drove his desire higher. She pushed her breast into his palm.

Their next kiss was deeper, hotter. The kind of kiss he'd been avoiding for the last three years. One where she felt like his, tasted like his.

"*Yes.*" She scraped her teeth along his jaw. "I've wanted you for so long, Ren."

She clung to him harder, and he kneaded the soft curves of her ass. Just a few layers separated them. What would her pretty pussy taste like? What would it feel like stretched around him?

Desire was tying him up in knots, he could barely think.

"I want you inside me," she breathed. "I ache for you. Only you can make it better."

"*Baby*." He took her mouth again. He rubbed her nipple between his fingers until it turned into a hard little nub.

Then he heard people talking nearby, followed by the *thunk* of gear hitting the deck.

And cold, icy reality intruded.

He stilled, his hands clenched on her.

Halle stiffened. "Ren...no."

He set her down on the bench, and pushed to his feet. He backed away from her and sliced a hand through his hair.

He'd come damn close to stripping her clothes off. *Halle. Tom's daughter*.

"Ren."

He looked up. Disappointment was stark on her face. He looked away, his gaze on the deck. His hands balled against his thighs. If he kept looking at her, he'd grab her, strip her clothes off, and be inside her before either of them could say anything else. His cock throbbed painfully.

"Lorenzo."

He met her gaze.

Her chin was high, stubborn determination on her face. "You feel it."

"Lust? Desire?" She had no idea the things he wanted to do to her. "The urge to fuck?"

She made an angry noise, and she stood. She took a step toward him, and Ren had to stop himself from taking a step back.

"Don't try to cheapen it," she said. "Our connection. We both care about each other. And yes, I want you to fuck my brains out."

He groaned. "*Halle*."

She took another step closer, her voice low. "No one has before."

His head whipped up.

"I've been waiting for you," she murmured. "And I'm not giving up on you."

He clenched his hand, flexed, then clenched it again. "I'm not good enough for you. I never will be."

She smiled. "It seems I have a thing for good men. Heroic ones who served their country. Who are strong and look out for others. Maybe I'm not good enough for you." She shrugged the blanket off and set it on the bench. Then she turned away. "Sweet dreams, Ren."

He watched her walk away, his gaze locked on the gentle sway of her hips as she disappeared down the deck.

He turned, and stared blindly at the dark ocean. But it didn't offer him any answers, didn't stop the scorching-hot need burning in his gut. He made his way back to his cabin. A few of the crew called out to him as he passed, and he managed a brief nod.

He slammed into his cabin.

It took him seconds to strip his clothes off, and he quickly shoved into the tiny bathroom. He turned on the shower, and made sure the water was cold.

His cock was still swollen and painful.

Halle was a virgin. No one had touched her.

He stepped under the icy spray, but it did little to cool him down.

No one had loved her, shown her pleasure.

He groaned, then circled his cock with one hand. He started stroking himself, rough, brutal. The water pounded over him.

Ren pictured her in his head—kissing her, her hands on him, fingers on his dick. His brain short circuited. He stroked his slick cock from root to tip. He jerked his arm hard and fast.

"Halle, shit, *Halle*." He imagined her small hand on his cock. Imagined working himself into her tight pussy.

He fucked his fist, until the rush of his climax hit. His back bowed and he shouted her name. He milked his cock, watching his come splash on the tiles. Pleasure was like a damn detonation inside him.

His knees nearly gave out and he slapped a hand to the tiles. "*Fuck*."

IT HAD BEEN A LONG DAY.

Halle headed across the deck, rubbing her temple. She hadn't slept well last night...again. The lack of sleep and hours in the sun were catching up with her.

Today, they'd been running more tests, and Ren had been conspicuously absent.

She lifted a hand and touched her lips. That kiss last night...

With a sigh, she turned to lean on the railing. She tried to take in the beautiful sunset, but she wasn't feeling it. She rubbed her eyes. It wasn't just because she was tired. It was because she was turned on, and wanting Ren.

He'd given her a taste of how it could be, and her body wanted more.

"Hey, Halle. You asleep standing up?"

Sammy's raspy voice made her jolt. She and Ryan appeared, flanking her.

"Almost. I didn't sleep well."

"Sleeping on a ship takes a bit of getting used to," Ryan said.

No, that wasn't her problem. Her problem was her body feeling hot and itchy. She'd tossed and turned, and thought of Ren.

Today, she'd worked extra hard to try and keep her mind busy on her work.

"How were the fuel cell tests today?" she asked.

"Excellent," Ryan said excitedly. "The professor is happy. You coming to dinner?"

Sammy nodded. "We're on our way to the mess now."

Halle shook her head. "I'll grab something later. I need to shower first." She waved to them, and headed to her cabin.

As she made her way down the narrow corridor, she glanced at the door to Ren's stateroom. She nibbled her lip and wondered if he was in there.

I'm not good enough for you.

His words had knocked around in her head all day. Did he really think that? He was a good man. She didn't pretend to understand things he'd done in the military, and the terrible things he'd no doubt seen. She'd seen her dad cope with his own issues when he'd come home from his deployments.

Serving his country just made her admire Ren more.

Back in her own cabin, she pulled her T-shirt off and kicked off her shorts. Her bra and panties followed. She needed a shower. Her mom always said things seemed better after a nice, warm shower.

Something niggled at Halle, and she paused. She turned and frowned. Why did her quarters suddenly feel weird? When she stepped into the bathroom, she noted that the cabinet above the sink was ajar.

She paused. She hadn't left it like that. It had been firmly shut when she'd left this morning. She snatched a towel off the rack, and wrapped it around herself.

She slowly opened the cabinet. Her toiletries had been moved. Her packet of painkillers and her asthma inhaler were turned around. Things hadn't been moved much, but enough for her to notice.

As though someone had been trying to put them back the way they'd found them.

She stepped back into her cabin, and looked around with a fresh gaze. Things on her desk were out of place. Her heart began to thump in her chest. The book on her bed was shifted. She yanked open the door to her narrow closet. A few shirts hung crookedly on their hangers.

Her breath hitched. Someone had been in her cabin.

Why?

She hadn't brought any valuables. Her pulse picked up speed. Could it be someone on the crew was a thief? Suddenly, Halle felt a little freaked out.

Someone had touched her things. Her clothes. Maybe her underwear.

She quickly opened the door and hurried down the hall. When she reached Ren's door, she lifted her hand and knocked.

It opened a second later. He frowned through the gap. "Halle?" When he saw her towel, his frown deepened.

"Ren. Someone's been in my cabin. It was locked when I left this morning. Things have been moved."

A hard, scary look crossed his face. He pushed past her and down the corridor.

Chest tight, she followed.

"Go back and wait in my cabin," he said.

"No. Whoever was there is gone now."

Ren stepped into her cabin, scanning around. He checked everything over. "You're sure things have been moved?"

She nodded, her skin feeling chilled. "Definitely. Someone tried to put it all back, but I have everything how I like it."

His lips quirked for just a split second. "You always liked things in the right place."

"Yes." What she wanted most was him with her. How could she get that through that thick shell of his? The look on his face made her shiver. "Ren? What are you thinking?"

"I'm thinking that someone on this ship searched your room, looking for something."

A chill skated over her skin. "Why? Looking for valuables? I didn't bring any money or jewelry."

He shook his head. "No. You're here working on a classified project. This has to be about the fuel cell. Add in someone trying to grab you before we left port..."

Halle felt sick. "But I told you, I'm not part of the main project."

Ren frowned. "You can access the data the others are collating, right? You can get the data on the fuel cell if someone demanded it?"

"Yes." She wrapped her arms around herself.

"I'll change the lock to the door and add an extra deadbolt." He took a step closer. "I won't let anyone hurt you."

"I know." She looked up at him. The room seemed to shrink. He was so big and took up so much space. She licked her lips.

"*Fuck.*" His head lowered a few inches. "I'm *not* touching you again."

"Are you telling me or yourself that?"

He growled. "Halle..."

"You won't touch me, even if I want you to?"

A muscle ticked in his jaw. "You know the reasons."

"Ren—"

He gripped her chin. "Find a boy your own age."

Anger shot through her. "A boy? I'm not a child. Is that what you really want? Me kissing someone else? Letting them touch me?"

A low growl escaped him.

Triumph filled her. "I didn't think so."

Then he spun. "Lock the door." He slammed it closed behind him.

Halle sagged against the wall. She was way out of her

league when it came to Ren Santoro, and she had no idea what to do about it.

REN TIGHTENED THE SCREW, then stepped back.

The new deadbolt on Halle's cabin door gleamed in the light. She was currently up in the mess having dinner, and he wanted this new lock installed before she got back. He tested it and frowned.

It still wasn't enough.

If someone wanted to get to her badly enough, they could. His jaw tightened. He thought again about someone searching Halle's cabin. Touching her things.

And the men who'd tried to snatch her at the bar before they'd left port.

Were the two things connected? His instincts told him yes.

And whoever had searched her cabin was aboard this ship. One of the crew or one of the research team couldn't be trusted.

It had to be related to the UUV and the fuel cell.

But if there was a link, he couldn't see it. Halle was a marine biologist, not an engineer.

A muscle ticked in his jaw. What he hated most was that whoever had searched her cabin was still on the ship.

Whoever the hell it was, Ren wasn't letting them get to Halle. They'd have to go through him first.

Heading up to the next deck, he stopped at the security office. It was a cramped space with a small weapons locker and two computers. Jack was sipping a mug of coffee and another of Ren's security team, Damien, was sitting in one of the chairs.

"Hey, Ren." Damien lifted his chin. He had dark skin, a bald head, and a big, muscular body. He'd played pro football for a year before a knee injury had ended his career. He'd joined the Army after that.

"We have an issue," Ren said.

Both men straightened, faces turning serious. Ren expected nothing less. He'd handpicked both of them for his team.

"Someone searched Halle's cabin. Jack, I need you to check the camera footage." They had a few security cameras in the common areas of the ship.

"On it." Jack spun and started tapping on the keyboard.

"Add this to someone trying to snatch her the night before we left port..." Ren shook his head. "I don't like it."

"You think it has something to do with this fuel cell?" Damien asked.

"I do."

Jack cursed. "Someone tampered with the video feed." He spun his chair around, looking pissed.

Ren crossed his arms over his chest. "So we have someone aboard this ship who can't be trusted. Someone with the skills to mess with our cameras." And they appeared to be targeting Halle.

"You're both on duty tonight. Keep a tight eye on that UUV. Be extra vigilant."

Both men stood and nodded.

"Whatever you need, Ren," Jack said.

After they'd left, Ren sank into one of the chairs and

sent a message on the computer. A few minutes later, it pinged with a reply. He tapped and a video call opened.

Even across the computer screen, the man radiated a dangerous intensity. Ren was well aware that Vander Norcross, his former Ghost Ops commander, was even more intense in real life.

He had Italian-American good looks with ink-black hair, dark stubble, and dark blue eyes. He ran Norcross Security in San Francisco, and despite falling in love and getting married, it sure hadn't softened his edge.

"Ren," Vander said. "Everything all right?"

"Thanks for taking my call, Vander."

"You know I'll always take your call. You're out at sea?"

"Yes." Ren blew out a breath. "Top secret project for the Navy."

Vander nodded. "UUV with some fancy fuel cell."

Ren laughed. "Is there anything you don't know?"

"Always like to keep my finger on the pulse. Problem with the testing?"

"No, the tests are going fine. Before we left port, masked men tried to grab one of the scientists on the research team. I stopped them, but I have no idea who was behind it. Then, today, someone searched her cabin."

A frown crossed Vander's face. "So someone on the ship is up to something."

Ren nodded. "I have to suspect they're after the fuel cell, and targeting Halle for some reason." He paused. "Vander, the marine biologist on the team is Halle. Halle Bradshaw."

"Your best friend, Tom's daughter. God, last I heard, she was in high school."

Ren cleared his throat. "She's working on this project as part of her post-graduate studies. She's twenty-three now."

"She's okay?"

"Shaken. But I'm not going to let *anything* happen to her."

Vander's gaze narrowed and Ren tried not to fidget. Vander was notorious for seeing things you didn't want him to see.

"What do you need, Ren?"

Relief hit him. He knew he could always depend on Vander, or any other members of his Ghost Ops team. "Can you get your guys to run background checks on all the members of the research team..." he drew in a breath "—and the *Atalanta* crew? Look for anyone who's gotten large payments or is in any trouble that could be exploited."

"You think it could be one of your crew?"

"I want to say no, but at this stage, I'm not ruling anyone out. I'll do whatever it takes to keep Halle safe." Ren cleared his throat. "And keep the UUV fuel cell secure."

"All right, leave it with me. If I find any red flags, I'll get back to you."

"Thanks, Vander. I appreciate it."

Vander lifted his chin. "You watch your back, and if you need anything else, call me." Vander's dark gaze met his. "Take care of your girl."

The screen went blank.

Ren sat back in his chair and checked his watch. On the security screen, he saw Halle heading back into her cabin. He saw her pause when she saw the new lock, then she disappeared inside.

He needed to grab some more coffee from the mess. Because he planned to spend the night in the hall outside Halle's cabin, making sure she was safe.

CHAPTER SIX

The *Atalanta* slowed to a stop. The sky was a stunning, clear blue, dotted with fluffy, white clouds. A pod of curious dolphins was swimming beside the ship.

Ren stood with his arms crossed, and watched the research team on the back deck of the ship. They were readying the UUV to go into the water for more tests.

He saw Ryan punch in a code and the side of the UUV opened. Ren could just make out the power cell.

It was smaller than he'd guessed, encased in a black box with some blinking lights on it.

Yes. This would re-revolutionize underwater drones. And plenty of people would risk a lot to get their hands on it.

He saw Halle step out on deck. Every muscle in his body went rigid.

She was wearing a wetsuit, but the top portion was hanging down around her waist. All she had on her torso was a small, red bikini top.

He shifted, willing his cock to behave. The fabric hugged her full breasts, and he could see the sweet curve of her belly. Her brown hair was up in a ponytail.

Before he realized what he was doing, he was heading down the steps toward her.

He saw people looking at her—the crew, her team members, fucking Ryan. Ren wanted to punch every one of them.

"What are you doing?" he bit out.

"Ren." She spun, pulling up her wetsuit and sliding her arms in.

At least she was covered now. His brain managed to start working again.

"I'm going to snorkel." She lifted up the mask she was holding. "There's a pod of dolphins out there. I want to see how they react to, and interact with, the UUV." She pointed to an underwater camera on the deck. It was in a special holder that would make it buoyant and easy for her to grip. "I'll take some photos, and I get to have a swim."

She'd always loved the water.

But they were in the middle of the ocean. He didn't love the idea of her being out there.

"Can't resist, can you, Ariel," he murmured.

She winked at him and headed down toward her team.

Ren's hands turned into fists, and he squeezed them until his knuckles turned white.

The professor waved to one of the crew, who activated the crane. The UUV lowered into the water. The rest of the team all huddled around a laptop, with Ryan at the controls.

"How's the power output?" Professor Davis asked.

"Steady," Ryan replied.

Then Halle dived in.

Ren dragged in a deep breath. She snorkeled on the surface. Some dolphins appeared, circling her. They were playful, and he heard her laugh.

Then a moment later she dived under the water. He could just make out her shadow.

He watched her swim and dive, taking photos, and getting farther away from the ship. He assumed she was photographing the drone and the dolphins.

There was also some flotsam in the water. Plastic. A sad reality of the ocean these days.

She dived under again, and he held his breath. A moment later, she came up.

Ren cupped his hands around his mouth. "Halle. There's debris in the water. Be careful."

"I see it," she called back. "There's more under the surface." There was disgust in her voice.

"How's the UUV?" Sammy called out.

"Looks great. I'm getting some good photos."

She dived under again.

Ren watched the dolphins. One leaped merrily into the air. The scientists were talking about the UUV results, and sounded excited. He tuned them out, and focused on the water.

Halle resurfaced, swimming alongside a dolphin for a little bit before she dived under again.

He leaned on the railing. They were two days into

the trip. They had three more days, and then they'd reach Hawaii.

Then she'd be gone.

His gut clenched. Yeah, he didn't like that, but he knew it was for the best.

The quicker they got to Hawaii, and Halle got off the ship, the better. He was doing what was right for her.

Something bobbed up out of the water.

Ren blinked and straightened.

"Oh my God, is that Halle's camera?" Sammy asked.

The team all moved to the railing. Everyone scanned the water. Heart pumping, Ren stared at the spot where he'd last seen her.

He suddenly noted that the dolphins were gone.

Halle.

Adrenaline pumped through his body. Something was wrong.

He kicked off his shoes, then ran across the deck. Without pausing, he dove off the back of the ship.

He hit, water closing over him. It was such a familiar feeling. He'd had intense training as a SEAL, and being in the water was second nature to him.

He sliced through the water. He reached the camera, then dove down deep.

There was good visibility. A second later, he saw the dolphins.

They were hovering right near where Halle was struggling in the water.

Her leg was caught in an old fishing net.

She was fighting and twisting, trying to get her leg free. As he watched, her movements turned sluggish.

No. Halle.

SHE WAS THRILLED with the photos she'd taken.

Halle swam closer to the dolphins. They made her smile. God, her mom would have loved this.

The shadow of the UUV was nearby, but she couldn't hear it. The team would be happy. She'd analyze the noise data later.

What didn't make her smile, however, was the debris in the water. It was probably waste dumped off cargo ships. There was trash, plastic, old fishing nets.

She took a big breath and dived deeper to take some more photos. The dolphins were curious about the UUV, and she watched one swim up to it.

She hovered in the water and snapped some more shots.

When she went to swim upward, she felt a tug on her leg.

She looked down. Her leg was caught in a fishing net.

Crap. She pulled, but she couldn't get free.

Adrenaline pumped into her system. She kept tugging, but the bottom half of her leg and her fin were wrapped in the netting.

She let go of the camera and it drifted upward. She grabbed at the net, trying desperately to free herself. She yanked, but the net just tangled tighter around her.

Tightness was building in her lungs. She bit down tighter on the mouthpiece of the snorkel. She wouldn't be able to hold her breath much longer.

Halle kicked harder. She was too deep for the others to see what had happened from their vantage point on the ship.

She spat the snorkel out, panic building. Bubbles escaped her mouth. Her lungs were starting to constrict and burn.

No. She had too much to live for.

Ren. She pictured his handsome face in her head.

She was starting to feel lightheaded, and soon she knew she wouldn't be able to stop herself from opening her mouth. Panic was hot and slick inside her.

Suddenly, a dark shape sliced closer.

Her heart hit her ribs. Then Ren was in front of her, still wearing his shirt and shorts. He had a fierce look on his face.

He touched her cheek, then kicked lower. She felt a hard tug on her leg.

Thank God. Her panic subsided. Ren was here. He'd get her out.

There was a giant tug. She was really dizzy now, and her lungs were burning.

Don't open your mouth. Don't open your mouth.

Then Ren wrapped his arms around her, and kicked. They shot toward the surface.

A moment later, their heads broke the surface.

Halle frantically heaved in air.

"You're okay, baby. I've got you. Just breathe."

His voice soothed her. He turned her so that her back was resting against his chest. She felt his warm lips against her cheeks.

"Lean back, and just breathe," he murmured in her ear.

Then he kicked. He pulled her back toward the ship. Each powerful kick sent them sailing through the water. Halle just relaxed against him and let him tow her.

Safe. She was safe now.

But before they reached the *Atalanta*, the shivers started. She felt so cold.

She'd almost died.

Worried faces on the deck peered down at her as they reached the ship. She closed her eyes. Ren handed her up, and two crew members pulled her aboard.

"You're okay, now," one man murmured. "We've got you."

Irrational panic trickled back into her system and she pulled away from the man. When Ren was holding her, she'd felt safe. Giant shivers wracked her.

"Halle, shit." Sammy arrived, wrapping a towel around her.

Fitz, Ryan, and Professor Davis hovered nearby, worry on their faces.

Ren climbed aboard. He was dripping water, and he yanked his wet shirt off.

Even with shivers overtaking her, she let her gaze run over his bronze skin and firm muscles.

"She needs to get warm," he said. "She's in shock."

"My camera—" Her voice shook.

"I don't give a shit about your camera," Ren said.

"We'll get it," Professor Davis said.

"Be careful of the debris." Ren reached down and

lifted her into his arms. "There are old fishing nets in the water. That's what she got tangled in."

Halle clung to him. He was so hard, so warm.

He strode down the main deck, and she buried her face against his neck. She sensed him going up the stairs and inside, the sun giving way to shadows.

She looked up and saw his jaw was tight. "You're mad at me."

"No. I'm mad that you almost..." His voice broke. "Just hold on, Halle. I'll get you warm. You're safe now."

"I know."

CHAPTER SEVEN

Ren carried Halle into his cabin. He kicked the door closed behind him with his foot.

She was shivering, and her face was pale.

She could've drowned. The thought drummed through his head.

He could have lost her.

His throat and chest were so damn tight. He knew the world would be a worse place without Halle's light in it.

"We'll get you warm, baby." He set her down on the bed, then ducked into the bathroom and started the shower. He turned the water to hot.

Back in his cabin, he saw her dragging in a deep breath, open hand pressed to her chest.

"Ren...I need my inhaler."

His pulse spiked. "Are you having an asthma attack?" He knew she'd had asthma as a kid. Her worst attacks had freaked Tom out.

She shook her head. "It's mild. I don't get attacks much anymore. My inhaler will help."

"I'll be right back." He hurried to her cabin and used his master key to get in. In her bathroom, he rifled through the cabinet and nabbed her inhaler.

She was still sitting on his bed when he returned. He handed her the inhaler, and she shook it and inhaled. Her shoulders relaxed, but a huge shiver wracked her.

"Let's get you warm, Ariel." He pulled her to her feet and started tugging off her wetsuit. Underneath, she was clad only in that maddening bikini. That, he was leaving on. He forced himself to ignore her sweet curves and bare legs, and focused on the goose pimples covering her skin.

"Come on." He urged her into the shower stall and under the water.

As he stepped back, her arm snapped out and she grabbed his wrist.

"Please don't leave me," she whispered.

Her wet hair was bedraggled, and she continued to shiver. Her cheeks were still paler than he would have liked.

Ren hesitated for a second, then without saying a word, he stepped under the spray. She needed him and he couldn't walk away. It was a tight fit in the stall, but he wound his arms around her.

She pressed her face to his chest.

God. He hugged her tightly. He held her until the shaking stopped.

"I was so scared," she murmured. "I thought no one would notice. I thought..."

"*Shh*. It's okay now. You're safe." He rubbed his chin on the top of her head.

Lifting a hand, he worked his fingers through her tangled hair. He reached out and grabbed some of his shampoo, squeezing some onto his palm. He massaged it into the strands of her hair.

It smelled like eucalyptus and mint, and he knew that she'd smell like him. He liked that more than he should.

He worked the dark strands of her hair through his fingers. She made a sound and tipped her head back. He tried not to notice the damp bikini clinging to her breasts, but it was hard. It left little to the imagination.

He tipped his gaze up to the tiles. *She nearly died, you asshole.*

"Warm now?" he asked.

"Yes."

He urged her back under the spray to wash the shampoo out. Happy now that she was warm, he turned off the shower. She stepped out onto the mat, and he grabbed a towel, drying her off. His heart was still pounding. His gut was tight, his jaw was tight.

He'd almost lost her.

He wrapped the towel around her, then quickly shed his wet cargo shorts and slung a towel around his waist.

He'd almost lost her. He dragged in a harsh breath.

"Ren."

He looked down into luminous blue eyes.

"I'm all right," she said. "You saved me."

He cupped her cheeks. "If I hadn't noticed you go under. If I'd been a few minutes later..."

"But you noticed, and you weren't later. I'm alive."

She let her towel drop to the floor, and touched his jaw, her fingers running along it. "But I'm cold."

"Let's get you in the bed, under the covers. That—"

"No," she said. "I...I need you to touch me. I need to feel warm again." She gripped his arms. "Make me forget the scary moments."

"Halle—"

She shuddered. "*Please*, Ren. Make me feel alive."

A part of him told him he should walk away. He shouldn't lay a finger on her.

But Halle needed him and that was all that mattered.

He stopped thinking. All he could do was feel, and make her feel better. He nudged her out of the bathroom, and across the cabin until she sat on the bed.

The wet fabric of her bikini clung to her curves. It made it hard for him to breathe. He reached back and untied the bikini top tied around her neck. Damn, his hand was shaking.

The fabric fell away, and he groaned. She was perfect. Every bit of her, from the dark-pink nipples, to the gentle curves of her breasts. Then she reached out and pulled his hand to her breast.

His fingers closed on her softness. Her nipple was hard, and her lips parted. He flicked a finger over that nipple.

She made a soft sound and pushed against his hand.

Each stroke, every hitch in her breath, reassured him that she was all right. "You're so beautiful, Halle. So perfect."

"I'm not perfect."

She was to him. He pushed her back on the bed, then

slid his palm over the curve of her belly. When he reached the tie side of the bikini, he toyed with it.

"*Ren.*" Her gaze was pleading.

And his control was gone. Like a rope ripped from his hands. He couldn't stop touching her. Hell, he didn't want to.

He untied the fabric and dragged it away.

Shit. Fuck.

"Look at you." He reached out and stroked his fingers through the neat, brown curls at the juncture of her thighs. He parted her legs, sliding his thumb through the pretty pink folds.

"*Oh.*" She arched. "Ren."

He wanted her warm, and shivering from pleasure, not cold and shock. He lowered his head, nuzzled her thigh.

"Anyone tasted you here before, Ariel?"

She shook her head.

"You going to let me put my mouth on you?"

She nodded.

"It's all mine, isn't it?" He slid his hand up her thigh.

She nodded again, pretty tits heaving. "Please put your mouth on me, Ren."

He pulled her legs over his shoulders and licked.

Her sweet, musky flavor hit him. He groaned, lapping at her.

Panting, she slid her hands into his hair. He growled, and shoved her thighs apart. He licked again, exploring her with his tongue.

"You taste so good, baby." He dragged his tongue

through her slick folds, then up until he found her clit. He used his tongue to tease her.

She writhed, panting his name. She tugged on his hair.

Fuck, he wasn't sure his cock had ever been this hard. He thrust his hips against the bed as he kept eating her. She was a feast he never, ever wanted to stop devouring.

"I'm...*God...*" Her words turned to a cry.

He looked up at her naked body and watched her come. He felt her pulsing against his mouth. She was pure beauty.

"Ren," she said breathlessly, slumping back on the bed.

He turned his face against her thigh. "Warm now?"

"Yes."

"Good."

But as his gaze moved over her naked body, taking in her flushed skin, guilt bit at him. The things he wanted to do to her...

Yeah, the guilt felt like sharp blades. All the reasons he shouldn't touch her ran through his head: Tom, her age, her innocence, his battered soul.

He rose. "I'll leave you to rest."

She pushed up on her elbows, frustration on her face. "Ren, don't go. Let's talk."

His laugh was harsh. "If I stay, we won't be talking."

Her gaze dropped down to the tented towel wrapped around his waist. It didn't do much to hide his raging erection.

"Don't go," she said again.

He turned and grabbed some dry clothes from his

closet. He slid into the bathroom, quickly pulled them on, and then headed for the door.

"Ren."

He glanced back at her. She sat in the center of his bed, naked, and looking impossibly young.

"I have to go." He shoved out of the cabin.

As he strode down the corridor, he raked a hand though this wet hair. He should never have touched her. Should never have put his mouth on her.

He stepped outside, and dragged in a breath. It didn't help that he could still taste her on his lips.

PROPPED up on the narrow bunk in her cabin, Halle balanced the laptop on her knees, and finished the analysis on today's data.

She was trying *not* to think about Ren.

Or about what had happened in his cabin today.

Halle made a frustrated sound and looked at the plain white ceiling. Okay, she hadn't stopped thinking about what had happened. The memory of his mouth on her, between her legs, eating her hungrily.

She squirmed on her bed. She'd come so hard. It had never been like that before. She'd touched herself, enjoyed a pleasant orgasm, but what she'd felt today...

She shivered and grabbed her glass of water off the built-in nightstand, and quickly sipped.

"Focus on your work, Halle," she muttered.

It had helped her not lose her mind this afternoon. One, from remembering the terrifying moments of being trapped in that net. And two, from remembering the way Ren had rushed out of that cabin. Away from her.

She sighed. God, the man confused her. Touching her like he couldn't get enough of her. Like he needed to touch her more than anything else. Then the next moment, leaving like he couldn't get away fast enough.

She rubbed her eyes with the heel of her hand. *Think about work.* She was almost done with the test data. And she'd sent off an email to her friends Conrad and Isabel. They'd studied together at college, and the pair had gone on to work on new technologies to clean the oceans of plastics. Halle had promised to donate her time and help them with their work after what she'd been through today.

There was a knock at her cabin door. Setting the laptop down on the bed, she cautiously approached the door. "Who is it?"

"Ms. Bradshaw, it's Kit from the mess." The muffled voice came through the door. "I have some food for you."

She recognized the voice of young man who cheerfully worked in the mess and galley. She unlocked the door, including the shiny new deadbolt Ren had installed, and opened the door.

Sandy-haired Kit stood with a covered plate, smiling widely at her.

"I was planning to head to the mess for dinner soon," she said.

"Ren asked me to deliver this." Kit whipped the cover off.

Halle gasped. "Oh, my gosh."

It was a plate filled with pink cotton candy. Several paper straws poked out of the cloud-like sweets.

Kit handed her the plate and leaned in. "Ren bullied the chef into making this for you, and getting it just right." The young man rolled his eyes. "Petrov was cursing in Russian, and Ren just stood there until he got it right."

Halle swallowed and stared down at the pink candy. "Thanks, Kit."

"You're welcome. And glad you're okay."

Halle closed the door with her hip, then sat on the bed. She lifted one of the cotton candy treats and took a big mouthful. The sweet goodness hit her taste buds and she grinned.

Ren. Her heart squeezed tight.

After gorging on too much cotton candy, Halle pulled a lightweight gray Scripps hoodie over her T-shirt and shorts. Then she headed for the mess.

Her team wasn't there yet, but several crew members were already eating. There was no sign of Ren. Halle filled her plate, trying to peer into the adjoining galley to catch a glimpse of Chef Petrov. She heard plenty of banging, crashing, and some cursing. Maybe she'd thank the chef later.

She sat at one of the tables and poked at her dinner.

"God, I'm so glad you're okay." Sammy dropped a tray of food onto the table beside Halle.

"Me too," Halle said quietly.

The team all sat around her. Only Ryan was missing.

"You feeling all right, Halle?" Fitz asked, a worried look in his eyes.

"I'm fine now, thanks." Fitz looked much healthier tonight. "How are you feeling?"

"Great. I'm starving." He forked a mouthful of mashed potato into his mouth.

Thankfully, it seemed his seasickness had eased.

Fitz chewed and swallowed. "Ren told me it would pass. He had me drinking some juice he'd made. Apple and carrot. Apparently, the sailors all swear by it."

How the man could think he wasn't a good guy was beyond her.

"Close call today." The professor gripped her shoulder and squeezed. "I'm glad you're all right, Halle."

"Thanks, Professor. After some rest, I'm feeling fine."

As her team all talked, Halle picked at her food. There was still no sign of Ren in the mess.

She sighed. She hadn't seen him at all since this morning. He was avoiding her. Again.

Sammy leaned closer. "The way your man dived in and rescued you." The other woman shivered. "Hot. I prefer girls, but I'd make an exception for him."

Halle flushed. "Keep your hands to yourself, Brooklyn."

Sammy laughed and held her hands up. "In all truthfulness, Halle, the man only has eyes for you. Remember, just be yourself."

"Well, I'm not sure that's working. He always takes off and avoids me."

In that moment, Fitz leaned over to ask Sammy about the day's test results.

Halle tuned them out, too lost in her head. So far, just being herself had sent Ren running. She rubbed her temple. The way he'd looked at her... Her stomach twisted into tiny knots, and she pushed her plate away. There was no way she could choke down more dinner.

"Halle," Sammy said. "I forgot to tell you. We recovered your camera, and I uploaded all the photos to the lab computer."

Halle smiled. Finally, some good news. She rose. "Thanks. I think I'll go and take a look at them. I'm behind because of today's drama."

"Don't overdo it, California," Sammy said.

Halle lifted her tray and headed over to the cleanup area, where she scraped off the plates and stacked them.

Then she walked out on the deck, down the stairs, and toward the lab. The night air was cool, and it washed over her flushed skin, making the ends of her hair dance.

She turned a corner on the stairs and ran into Ryan.

"Hey, Halle, you all right?" He gripped her shoulders.

"I'm doing fine. Thanks."

"Today was scary as hell for me, so I'm guessing it was worse for you." He squeezed her shoulder. "If you need company tonight—"

She stepped away. "Thanks, Ryan. I appreciate the concern, but I'm okay. I'm going to do some work."

He reached up and rubbed the back of his neck. "Look Halle, I like you."

She sighed. "I know. I like you too, but only as friends and coworkers."

His face tightened. "Okay, message received."

She hoped he was being truthful, but something told

her Ryan didn't like hearing no for an answer. She nodded. "Night."

As she walked to the lab, the back of her neck prickled. Slowing, she turned and scanned the main deck. It was empty.

But night had fallen and there were plenty of dark shadows.

She was sure someone was watching her.

It's just nerves, Halle. You've had an interesting day. She opened the door and headed into the lab. She flicked all the lights on.

She opened a laptop, and quickly got to work finding the photos. She hoped she'd gotten some good ones. She copied them over to a flash drive. She'd take them back to her cabin and work on them there.

Once she had the information, she closed the laptop and slipped the flash drive into her pocket. She cautiously stepped out of the lab.

She paused for a second. This time, there was no creepy sensation of being watched. She blew out a breath. She'd been imagining things.

"See, all good." She strode down the deck. While she'd been in the lab, the temperature had dropped. Goosebumps prickled on her bare legs. "You're fine, Halle. You just had a rough day."

Magnificent orgasm aside, of course.

No, she wasn't thinking about orgasms or Ren right now.

She found herself wandering toward the back of the ship. The night sky was amazing. She paused and looked up at the stars overhead. A sense of wonder filled her, and she savored the moment. They were beautiful. She hoped her mom was up there, enjoying the glittering light.

She turned to head for the stairs. *Movement.* She frowned and squinted toward the ship's stern. A shadow was moving near the submersibles.

Right near where the UUV was stored.

CHAPTER EIGHT

It was a nice night. A cool breeze ruffled Ren's hair as he stared out over the water.

He'd avoided Halle. Again.

He could almost hear his Ghost Ops buddy Shep calling him a fucking coward.

He shouldn't have touched her in the first place. He shouldn't have put his hands and mouth on her. He closed his eyes. He was still half hard. The sounds she'd made...

"*Fuck.*"

He had to get a grip on this or he'd have her under him, and guaranteed, she wouldn't be a virgin anymore.

He blew out a breath. Then he heard a shout.

"Hey!"

He straightened instantly. It was Halle.

He charged down the stairs and hit the main deck at a run. It sounded like she was at the ship's stern.

"Get away from that," she cried.

Ren circled one of the submersibles, moving fast.

Then he saw her. She was wearing shorts and a gray hoodie.

Then, beyond her, he spotted movement; a dark shadow.

Right near the UUV.

Ren picked up speed, and watched as the shadow darted away.

"Halle?" he called out.

She whirled, relief filling her face. "Ren. Thank God. There was someone by the drone."

He scanned the deck. No way in hell he was leaving her alone.

"What's the commotion?" Ryan appeared, followed by Sammy and Fitz. Several of the crew members arrived, as well.

"You're okay?" Ren asked Halle.

She nodded.

"Did you see who it was?"

She shook her head. "It was too dark."

He spotted Jack and Damien. He jerked his head, and his men nodded. They disappeared into the darkness as they started searching the deck.

"Someone was out here," Halle told her team. "Near the UUV."

Ryan cursed and surged forward. He leaned over the drone storage case. It was open, the drone on full display.

"*Dammit*. Look," he said. "Someone was trying to open the panel on the UUV."

Ren stepped closer. The metal of the UUV was scratched.

"Shit." Ryan dropped down to his knees, hands

running over the drone. "That's the housing for the fuel cell."

"What's going on?" Professor Davis stepped into view, frowning.

A crowd had gathered. Ren stared at the spot where the shadowy figure had disappeared.

It was someone who was on the ship.

"Someone tried to get the fuel cell," Ren said.

The professor's brow creased. "What?"

"I yelled out," Halle said. "It must have scared them off."

"Ren, we need to increase security," the professor said. "The fuel cell *must* be protected at all costs."

"On it. My men are already searching for any clue as to who it was."

The professor blew out a breath and ran a hand through his hair.

Ren looked back down at the scratch marks. "Whoever it was, they weren't able to get it, at least."

Ryan shook his head. "The panel is protected by a sophisticated lock. You can only open it with the right code."

"Who has the code?" Ren asked.

"Ryan and I," Professor Davis said. "And one backup member of our team."

Cold trickled down Ren's spine. "And Halle."

She nodded. "I'm just a backup in case Ryan and the professor are unavailable."

Things clicked in Ren's head. Someone had tried to grab her back in San Diego, someone had searched her cabin. They were after the code.

"And you're sure you didn't see the guy?" he asked her.

"Sorry." She held up her hands. "It was just too dark. He was just a shadow."

"Tall? Short?"

She grimaced. "Medium height."

That described half the men on the ship.

Jack and Damien reappeared. Ren strode over to join them. "Anything?"

Jack shook his head. "A couple of smudged footprints on the deck. Nothing to identify them."

"I'll check the cameras when I get back to the security office," Damien said. "But it looks like whoever it was knew where they were, and stuck to the shadows."

Ren's mouth flattened. "I want round-the-clock security on the UUV. Get more lights out here as well. I don't want any shadows for people to lurk in."

"You got it, boss," Jack said.

"Damien, set up a hidden camera no one will spot. I want it pointed directly at the UUV."

The tall man nodded.

Ren turned to the crowd. "Okay, everyone turn in, now. The drone's secure. Time to get back to your duties or your cabins."

People drifted away, murmurs of conversation fading, until only Halle was left.

"You sure you're all right?" he asked.

She shoved her hands in the kangaroo pocket of her hoodie. "I went to the lab, and I felt someone watching me. I thought I was just imagining it."

His jaw tightened.

"Then when I came out, I saw someone by the UUV." She shivered.

Ren rubbed his hands up and down her arms. "You're safe." *No one* was hurting her. "You're not going anywhere by yourself from now on. Make sure you have someone with you at all times. And make sure that you use that extra lock I installed on your cabin door."

She wrapped her arms around herself. "There's no way I'll sleep tonight. Not after this, and this morning..."

Ren knew he should walk away. His jaw tightened and he looked out at the dark water.

"I didn't get a chance to thank you for the cotton candy, since you were busy avoiding me."

He looked back at her. "I figured we both needed some space."

"I don't need space, Ren." She sucked in a breath. "Anyway, thanks for the cotton candy. It made me feel better."

He couldn't take his gaze off her face.

"I guess I should get back to my cabin. I have photos to go through, so hopefully that'll help take my mind off things."

He took her hand, then he towed her behind him down the deck.

"Ren? Where are we going?"

"No questions."

He couldn't stand the idea of her alone in her cabin—worried, scared, upset. And with everything going on, Ren had a really bad feeling.

It was his job to keep her safe, and the best way to do that was to not let her out of his sight.

He led her to his stateroom. She hovered just inside the door while he leaned over and turned on his television. He quickly cued up the show he wanted from his collection.

All he wanted to do was get her mind off everything. He wanted to see her smile.

He wanted to reassure himself that she was alive and safe.

The screen flickered, and the black-and-white show started.

Her face lit up. "*Flash Gordon*?"

"Only the best." He lay down on the bed, propping pillows under his head, before he patted the covers beside him.

She dropped down on the bed, and snuggled against him.

"Maybe we can watch the 80s movie version later too," he said.

She laughed. The sweetest damn sound. "I know you like that better, but it's so corny."

"And this isn't?"

"This is a classic, Ren."

As the old sci-fi show played, he watched her mouth the words. He was well-aware that she knew every bit of this one off by heart.

He kept her tucked against his side. Damn, she felt good there. *Right*.

For tonight, he wasn't going to overthink everything.

He'd make sure she slept tonight. And he'd make sure she was safe.

HALLE BLINKED AWAKE.

Mmm. She was warm and cozy. A hard, muscular arm was wrapped around her. Her heart bumped against her chest. She was lying on her side, and held tight against Ren.

He was lying on his back, still asleep. Her heart did a little crazy dance. God, he was so gorgeous. A big, male animal. Her gaze ran over the lean muscles of his bare chest.

She felt so safe with him.

She'd slept like a rock through the night. Not once had she woken up. Not once had she worried about anything.

It had been a long time since she'd felt like that. She realized that losing her mother had shaken her sense of safety and security. She'd learned that the world could be hard and tough.

That everything could change in an instant.

A dog could run in front of your car. A net could wrap around your leg. A man could kiss you and change everything.

Nuzzling against Ren's skin, she breathed in his scent. She wanted to enjoy this moment, before he woke up and told her all the reasons why they couldn't be together.

His hand tightened on her, and squeezed her hip.

"Hey." His voice was husky from sleep.

She cleared her throat. "Good morning."

He slid a hand into her hair. "Feel okay?"

"I'm fine, Ren."

She was mostly fine. She was still worried about whoever had tried to get the fuel cell.

Callused fingers rubbed along her jaw, and her pulse jumped. Suddenly, her belly felt hot and tingly.

"Did you sleep all right?"

"Best sleep I've had." She met his gaze. "Is this where you run away?"

"I should."

"Ren..." She swallowed. "I've made it clear how I feel about you. If you don't feel the same way I do..." Her throat was so tight. "If you don't want me as much as I want you..."

The hand in her hair cupped the back of her skull. His brown eyes looked molten hot. "I do. That's the problem."

Oh. "It doesn't need to be a problem. I'm not a child. And my father loves you." *I think I could fall in love with you, too.*

"Damn you, Halle. For being so beautiful." He pulled her down for a kiss.

As their lips meshed and tongues tangled, all she could think of was Ren.

Suddenly, he sat up with a flex of muscles, pulling her closer. "You're pure temptation," he growled. "I can't resist you."

"Stop thinking and just feel," she said against his lips.

He angled his head and took the kiss deeper. He sucked on her bottom lip, then plundered her mouth with his tongue.

Oh. Yes. She kissed him back, tasting every bit of his

gorgeous mouth. His tongue glided over hers, and she cupped his cheeks, loving the rough feel of his stubble.

She moved against him, desperate to feel more.

"You hungry, baby?" he murmured.

"Yes. For you."

He slid a hand between her legs, and she cried out.

"You're soaked." His fingers flicked along the edge of her panties. She rubbed against him, riding his hand.

"You want my mouth on you again?" His voice was low and deep.

"Yes. But I want to touch you, too." She slipped a hand between them and pressed it to the bulge in his boxer shorts.

He groaned. "Naughty." Suddenly, he spun her over his lap. She gasped, loving how strong he was. His hand smoothed over her ass, then he pushed up the T-shirt she'd borrowed from him, baring her butt. His hands caressed her buttocks.

"*Ren*," she said breathily.

He pulled her panties down, then slid a hand between her thighs, stroking her pussy.

"This ass." He kneaded one cheek. "It's always teasing me."

The slap took her by surprise. "Oh." The feel of his palm made her squirm and heat shot through her.

"You like that?" he murmured.

"Yes."

"You're naughtier than I thought, baby." He slapped her other buttock.

Halle jolted and bit her lip. Then he stroked between her legs again. *Oh, God.*

"I'm going to make you come." He pushed a finger inside her and she moaned. "Damn, so tight."

In, then out. His finger delved deeper, and his thumb found her clit. Electricity whipped through her, zapping between her legs, up her spine. He kept touching her, leaving her shaking. Her hands twisted in the sheets.

The sounds she made now were incoherent. All she could feel was the heat inside her, every muscle in her body shivering.

He eased his finger out, toying with her clit, then when he pushed back inside her, he added a second finger.

She rocked against his hand. She teetered on the precipice. She wanted to come, needed it.

"*Ren*."

"That's it, Halle. Come on my fingers. I want to feel you come."

She squeezed her thighs together, trapping his hand, as her release hit. She screamed his name. Liquid heat drenched her core as her body shook. The pleasure left her dizzy.

"Fuck, so beautiful." He rolled her over and she watched as he sucked the fingers he'd had inside her into his mouth.

Dazed, she watched him. "Please. I want to give you pleasure, too. This time, let me touch you."

His face looked harsh, set in lines of desire and conflict. Her heart squeezed, and she was sure that he was going to push her away again.

"On your knees, pretty girl."

Her heart soared. Halle wriggled off the bed. She

nestled between his muscular legs, her gaze locked on the large bulge in his boxer shorts. She pushed the cotton down, and his hard cock sprang free. It was as beautiful as the rest of him; long, thick, and so swollen.

"Halle..."

She gripped him with one hand, fingers flexing on him. He felt like hot steel. When he groaned, need shot through her.

She leaned forward and put her mouth on his cock.

He uttered a curse.

She licked, sucking at the fluid leaking from him. He was thick and she opened her mouth wider, took him deeper.

"God, look at your pretty lips stretched around my cock." His voice was strained, guttural. He slid a palm into her hair. "Look at me corrupting that innocent mouth."

She pressed her hands to his thighs, moaning as she moved. She went deeper, and choked a little. Eyes watering, she kept sucking his cock, wanting to give him as much pleasure as he'd given her.

Flicking her gaze up, she saw him watching her. The look on his face filled her with power. She sucked harder and hollowed her cheeks, taking his length deeper.

"Oh, shit," he growled.

She loved him in her mouth. He felt amazing. Tasted amazing.

As she kept working him, every sensation felt magnified—the low growls he made, the way his hips jerked, the way his fingers tightened in her hair.

She wanted to take him all the way, and watch him come. For her. Because of her.

"Halle, I'm going to come." His hand clenched on her hair. "Pull up, baby."

When he tried to pull back, she moved forward and sucked his cock harder. She slid one hand up his thick thigh and dug her nails in.

He groaned deeply, and pumped his big cock into her mouth. As he came, he growled her name, and she swallowed his load. Everything he had.

His cock had just started to soften when he pulled her up. "Damn, Halle. You destroy me." He kissed her, hard.

She hugged him. "I don't want to destroy you." No, she wanted to put him back together. Make him realize there was so much more he could have.

She wanted to be a part of his whole.

CHAPTER NINE

Ren helped Ryan connect the UUV to the *Atalanta's* crane.

"Thanks," Ryan said.

Ren nodded. "We had extra security on it all night. There were no problems." He eyed the younger man, wondering if he could be behind the attempts on the fuel cell. He hadn't heard anything from Vander yet.

Ryan put his hands on his hips, looking troubled. "We can't let the fuel cell fall into enemy hands."

"I know." Ren turned his head and saw Halle on the deck. The bikini was blue today, and she was wearing a wetsuit again.

She saw him and smiled.

He felt that smile in his chest, God, and his cock.

Now that he'd touched her, he couldn't stop. Holding her in his arms all night had been the best thing he'd experienced in a long time. Having her mouth on his cock...

He blew out a sharp breath. After she'd blown his

damn mind, they'd both quickly showered and dressed for the day. She'd been due to meet her team, and he'd had to check in with his men.

"You're not just a family friend to her."

Ryan's voice made Ren jerk his head around.

The man pulled a face. "Family friends don't look at each other the way you look at her."

"She's special."

"I know. I'd really hoped to convince her to date me."

Ren's mouth flattened.

"But she's made it clear she's not interested," Ryan continued. "Now I know why."

Ren lifted a brow.

"She's in love with you."

Love? The word was like a fist in Ren's gut.

Ryan laughed. "You just went pale."

"She's too young for me."

Ryan snorted. "She doesn't think so. Besides, once you're an adult, there are no rules that say how old you have to be to be with someone. I'd do anything to be with her."

Ren narrowed his gaze.

"Cool it with the death stare." Ryan held up his hands in mock surrender. "Halle and I are just friends. Like I said, she's made that very clear."

The ugly pressure inside Ren eased a little.

"Treat her right," Ryan said. "Take care of her." With a nod, the scientist turned away.

Ren watched the man walk away. Right now, he needed to focus on keeping both Halle and the fuel cell safe. Not just on wondering when he could touch her again.

The research team got busy getting the UUV into the water for the next test.

He and his security team had swept the ship and checked out all the security footage. There was nothing to point them to the identity of whoever was after the fuel cell. The rest of the night had been uneventful. Damien had set up the hidden camera to watch the UUV, and any movement would trigger an alert to Ren's phone. He was one of the few aboard connected constantly to the ship's satellite Wi-Fi.

Halle walked past Ren, her fingers dragging across his abs. He grabbed her hand.

She looked back over her shoulder, a teasing glint in her blue eyes. He squeezed her fingers.

"Tell me you aren't going in the water today," he said.

"I am. It's my job. I'll be more careful, and don't worry, I have this." She patted the knife he'd given her this morning. It was attached to her belt.

The SRK SK-5 was one of the knives he'd used when he was in Ghost Ops. Knowing she had it, felt right.

He nodded, but he'd still watch her like a hawk.

She headed down to the back deck, talking with the rest of the team. He heard her laugh.

He knew he wasn't good enough for her. She'd seen some of his broken pieces, but there were more. And they weren't pretty.

He was going to break her heart.

Tom would never forgive him. He'd never forgive himself.

Captain Shroff appeared at the railing beside him, scattering his thoughts.

"We're not far from Hawaii now," Jay said. "The tests have gone well."

"They have. But I'm worried about whoever was poking around the drone last night."

The captain stroked his beard. "Me too. Have you and your team had any luck working out who it might be?"

"No." Frustration cut through Ren. "I'm doing some digging. If it's someone working for a foreign country or group, there'll be signs." He paused. "Jay, it could be one of our crew."

The captain's face hardened. "If it is, they'll be punished. I'm glad we'll reach port tomorrow, and that UUV will be off my ship."

Ren nodded.

Then what? Was he going to let Halle walk away?

Fuck. He couldn't.

She deserved to know how special she was. He couldn't be an asshole and keep pushing her away. He'd accused her of being too young, and she was the one acting like the adult.

Fucking hell. He needed to talk to Tom. The thought made his gut turn over.

Then, down below, he watched Halle dive gracefully into the water.

Could he watch her walk away from him?

He wasn't strong enough to do that.

Every instinct he had screamed at him to keep her. To hold her and keep her safe.

IT HAD BEEN A LONG DAY.

A busy day. Halle hadn't seen much of Ren, although she didn't think he was actually avoiding her today. He'd watched her the entire time she'd been in the water, and anytime she'd caught his gaze, he'd smiled at her.

After that, when she had seen him, he'd seemed distracted. Not like a man excited to see the woman he'd made come hard the night before.

She sighed. She knew things hadn't been easy for him, and relationships weren't really something he did. His childhood had been tough, with no dad on the scene. He'd been raised by his mom and grandmother, and almost pulled into gang life.

She'd heard him say that the military was the best thing that ever happened to him, but she knew it had stripped away bits of his soul. Losing people did that, too.

Halle leaned on the railing and watched the moonlight glimmer on the water. Maybe she was naïve in thinking she could make him want her the way she wanted him.

Maybe she was hurting him more in the process. Making him so conflicted about being with her.

With a shake of her head, she headed to her cabin. A shower would help. And she *wasn't* going to think of the shower she'd shared with Ren.

She unlocked her cabin door and pulled off her hoodie.

There was a piece of paper lying in the center of her bed.

Weird. She didn't remember leaving that there.

Frowning, she snatched it up and unfolded it.

Write the fuel cell code on the back of this paper, and leave it at the front of the ship in the blanket box.

Do it, or you'll go overboard, and no one will know.

Her chest locked, and it was hard to breathe. She stared blindly at the dark, bold letters.

Tell anyone and you die.

Do as you're told, and you live.

Her hands shook, causing her to crumple the paper. *Who the hell was doing this?*

It had to be one of the crew members. Maybe they'd been bribed? It couldn't be one of her co-workers.

She needed to tell Ren. She pulled her hoodie back on and put the note into her pocket. As she walked down the hall, her heart started beating hard. If anyone saw her...

She knocked quietly on Ren's door.

He opened it, just wearing a T-shirt and shorts, his face impassive.

"Ren..."

His face changed. "What's wrong?"

"Please, let me in."

He nudged the door wider, and she slipped inside. Then she whirled, her hands feeling so cold. She pulled the note out and handed it to him.

As he read it, she watched rage grow on his face.

He dropped the note on his desk and grabbed her hands. "No one is going to hurt you."

"I know... God, who's doing this?"

"I'll find out." His voice had gone into scary territory. "Your door was locked?"

She nodded. "Ren, I'm freaked out."

He chafed his hands up and down her arms. "I promise I'll protect you."

"But I want you safe as well. We've got no idea who's behind this. Or how dangerous they are."

He cupped her face. "Halle."

Then he kissed her.

A second later, the kiss went wild. Tongues stroked, they grabbed at each other. He spun and pinned her to the wall. She desperately tried to get closer, biting his jaw.

"You're all I think about," she whispered.

"I can't get you out of my head."

"Stop fighting this," she whispered. "Us. Stop fighting us."

He made a sound. Then he released her and whirled away. "Fuck, Halle, do you want me to break your heart?"

She lifted her chin. "You can't."

"I'm not the love and relationships kind of guy. Maybe once I was capable of it, but not now. I *will* break your heart."

"Try it."

His face twisted. "You're so fucking stubborn."

"So are you." She moved closer.

With a sigh, he pulled her close. "Damn you, Halle." He pressed his mouth to hers. This kiss was slow and gentle. He lifted his head. "I need to talk to my security guys about the note. Stay here."

"Are you sure you can trust them? Are you sure we can trust anyone on the ship?"

His face turned grim. "I don't know yet, but I know Jack wouldn't have anything to do with this. I've known him for years. I'll just talk with him. Stay here."

"All right. Just stay safe and come back to me safely."

AS JACK LEFT the security office, Ren locked the door and sat in front of the computer. Like him, Jack hadn't been happy about the note.

Things were escalating and Ren didn't like it.

A window popped up on the computer screen and Ren leaned forward. "Vander."

On the screen, Vander nodded. "I don't have anything definitive for you, Ren. We're still running all the background checks. It doesn't help that the *Atalanta's* crew come from countries all around the world."

"You haven't found any red flags?"

"A few people with gambling debts, and ex-wives they pay money to, but nothing outside what they can cover with their salaries and investments."

"And the research team?"

"Ryan Hughes had a large sum deposited into his bank recently."

Ren straightened.

Vander held up a hand. "Don't get excited. Ace traced it. It was an inheritance from his grandfather. Mark Davis is clean to the point of being extremely boring. Samantha Sorvino and Fitz Armstong are clear."

Ren's pulse started pounding. "And Halle?"

Vander leaned back in his chair, his face impassive. "She makes regular monthly payments to an offshore account. Just a few hundred dollars, but it's like clockwork. The account is for a company called Bright Blue, but Ace hasn't been able to track who owns the account or what Bright Blue does. Figured I should mention it."

"She's paying someone?" Ren frowned.

"Could be blackmail. Could be to fund something she doesn't want anyone to know about."

Ren shook his head. "*No.* Halle has nothing to do with whoever is after the fuel cell. Someone is targeting *her*."

"I'm just sharing what we've found, Ren. I know she's important to you."

"Shit, Vander." Ren sliced a hand through his hair. "I should never have touched her. I...she's under my damn skin."

"Women, the right ones, tend to do that." Vander's lips quirked.

"She's young, innocent, so damn good. There is no way in hell I'll ever deserve her."

Now his friend's mouth flattened. "You are a good man, Ren. One who risked his life for his country, and did a lot of shit so other people didn't have to. I know what happened to Nasrin still haunts you."

Ren pressed his lips together, the sound of his heartbeat echoing in his head.

"It was tragic, but not your fault."

"I still hear her screams, Vander. I will never, ever

forget that little girl." A girl who'd died because her father had helped Ren.

"Don't forget her, but don't dishonor her life by not letting yourself live yours."

Ren shook his head. He couldn't focus on the past right now. "I need to find out who aboard the *Atalanta* wants that fuel cell and why."

Vander nodded. "We'll keep digging. As soon as I know something, I'll be in touch. You'll reach Hawaii soon?"

"Tomorrow."

"Ren, if you need back up, you know Sawyer is on Maui. He's a deputy sheriff there now."

Sawyer Lane was another former Ghost Ops buddy. He'd only gotten out of the military in the last year, and taken a job as a deputy sheriff in Hawaii. It was the perfect job for him because Sawyer was steady as a rock, protective, and had the patience of a saint.

"I hope I don't need his help. Thanks, Vander."

"Be careful, Ren."

Ren closed down the computer and headed back to his cabin. He found Halle pacing.

When she saw him, her shoulders sagged, and relief crossed her face. "Did you find anything?"

He shook his head and sat on the bed. He patted the spot beside him.

She studied his face, then sat. "What's wrong?"

He took her hand. "I asked a friend of mine to run some checks...on everyone aboard this ship."

"Okay. Did your friend find anything?"

"Nothing that tells me who's after the fuel cell." Ren

paused. "I do have a question for you. Why do you pay money into an offshore account each month?"

Her eyes went wide. "Wow. Your friend is really doing some digging."

Ren growled. "Halle."

"Wait. You think I'm the one after the fuel cell." She shot to her feet. "Ren, apart from my father, you know me better than anyone. I—"

He gripped her hips. "I don't think you're after the fuel cell."

She eyed him. "Well, I'm happy to know you don't think I'm a traitor or a terrorist."

He tugged her into his lap. "What's Bright Blue?"

"It's a start-up developing technologies to rid the ocean of plastic waste. Two friends I went to college with started it. Conrad and Isabel are out to save the ocean. They're doing good work and after my little incident, I'll also be donating my time when I can to help them."

Ren pressed his forehead to hers. "You going to save the world, Ariel?"

"One part of it, at least." She yawned and slapped a hand over her mouth. "Sorry."

He hugged her. "I think it's time to get some sleep."

Her nose wrinkled. "Are you sending me back to my cabin?"

"No. You're staying right here." Where he could keep her safe.

CHAPTER TEN

It was the middle of the night and Ren was still awake.

Halle was nestled against him, sleeping soundly. She'd been shaken by the note, and it had taken her a while to fall asleep. But he'd held her until she settled.

Someone aboard the *Atalanta* was after the fuel cell. That thought kept reverberating in his head.

He'd vetted every crew member himself when they were first hired, but it was impossible to know if someone had money issues, or some other personal issue that a foreign country or terror group could put pressure on.

If it wasn't one of the crew, it had to be one of the research team. He frowned. But Vander hadn't found anything yet. And why would one of the team sabotage their own project. Money? Blackmail?

It did make sense for them to target Halle, so they could use her code to open the fuel cell, and throw suspicion off themselves.

Damn, he hated not knowing.

Tomorrow, they'd dock in Hawaii. Then the UUV would be safely off the ship.

Halle made a noise in her sleep, turning restlessly. He stroked her back and she relaxed again.

Looking after her, being with her, felt so easy. She made him feel so damn much.

He stared up at the darkened ceiling. He hadn't wanted to feel. He blew out a breath. After he'd left the military, he hadn't wanted to feel anything.

Being out on the ocean... Hell, it was his way of avoiding people. A way to avoid deeper connections.

God, he'd given Shep a hard time for living up on his Colorado Mountain alone, avoiding people and relationships. Ren tightened his hold on Halle. Meanwhile, Ren had been doing his own version of the same thing.

And when he'd kissed a sweet, beautiful woman on her twentieth birthday, it had ignited so much emotion that he'd run even farther and faster.

Maybe it was time to stop running.

Suddenly, he heard a vibration.

Frowning, he saw his phone glow on the built-in nightstand. Careful not to jostle Halle, he grabbed it.

And saw an alert for the hidden camera.

Fuck. Something had activated it. His heart kicked in his chest, and he swiped the screen.

A shadowed image appeared on the screen. He saw the UUV storage case in the center of the image.

And three silhouettes of big men in wetsuits moving across the deck.

Ren sat up. They'd been boarded.

Halle stirred. "Ren? What's wrong?" she asked sleepily.

Shouts reverberated on deck. He tensed.

Bang. Bang. Bang.

His blood turned ice cold.

Gunfire.

Halle jerked upright. "Oh, my God, what was that?"

He cupped her face. "That was gunfire. Get dressed. Fast."

"*God.*" Her voice was a harsh whisper.

Ren quickly dressed and pulled out his two handguns from the lock box in his closet. He slid them into his waistband.

He had no idea what was happening on deck. He grabbed his waterproof backpack, and shoved some essentials into it. There was a chance he might need to get Halle off the ship.

He turned and saw she was dressed in a long-sleeved T-shirt, shorts, and running shoes.

"Stay close. We need to get on deck and see what's going on."

She looked scared, but she swallowed and nodded.

He pressed a quick kiss to her lips.

They slipped out of his stateroom and down the corridor, moving quickly to the stairs.

More shouts sounded below, and then someone screamed. He led her down, staying close to the wall.

He almost tripped over a body at the base of the stairs. *Damn.*

Ren saw the *Atalanta* shirt and shifted to see the man's face.

Fuck. It was his man, Jack. He had a bullet hole in his forehead.

"Oh, no," Halle breathed. Her hand clenched on his arm.

Ren's jaw throbbed. He forced his churning emotions down. He had to get Halle safe, then he could find justice for Jack.

He tugged her down the deck, keeping her behind him.

And came face-to-face with a man in a black wetsuit and mask.

Ren let instinct take over. He attacked—hard and fast. He landed a hard kick to the man's midsection, and followed through with several punches. The man grunted.

Ren had to protect Halle. He launched into another flurry of blows.

Wetsuit guy pulled a knife. He swung at Ren, but Ren ducked, and rammed the man into the wall. He gripped the man's arm, turning the blade back to face the attacker. They strained, their muscles burning as the battle turned into one of pure strength.

And determination.

Ren had too much to fight for.

The man grunted, but Ren shoved, and the knife bit into the man's chest.

"You picked the wrong ship to attack," Ren muttered.

The knife slid between the man's ribs. He made a gurgling sound, then sagged.

Ren stepped back, chest heaving. The man slid down

the wall, leaving a trail of blood. Halle stood nearby, wide-eyed.

Shit, she'd just watched him kill a man.

Again, he locked his emotions down. "Come on." He held out his hand.

She didn't hesitate to take it. That was something, at least. They hurried toward the stern of the ship, staying close to the hulks of the submersibles. He knew there were other intruders in wetsuits aboard the ship.

He heard shouts and pulled Halle to a stop. Hunched under the *Atalanta*'s largest submersible, he peered around. His teeth clicked together.

Some of the crew had been rounded up. They were on their knees, hands behind their heads, with several armed, black-clad intruders guarding them.

"They're after the fuel cell," Halle whispered.

"Yeah."

"Ren, we can't let them take it."

The soldier in Ren warred with the man in him. The man wanted to protect Halle and get her far away from danger. The soldier wanted to protect the fuel cell.

He released a heavy breath. "Come on." He pulled her around the back of the submersible. He was careful to stick to the shadows. When they reached the very back of the ship, he spotted another man in a wetsuit, searching all the boxes.

They didn't know where the UUV was. Hell, they'd walked right past it when they'd boarded.

"Stay here."

She nodded.

Ren crept up silently. In Ghost Ops, it was what

they'd been best at. Sneaking deep into enemy territory, moving through the shadows, with no one knowing they were just inches away.

They'd been ghosts.

The man in the wetsuit didn't hear him coming.

He attacked the man from behind, sliding an arm over his neck. Ren yanked him back hard, cutting off his air.

The man was tough, he jerked his body, feet hammering the deck. *Fuck*, Ren hoped no one heard him. He tugged harder. The asshole managed to ram an elbow back into Ren's ribs. He grunted and ignored the pain.

The man tried to pull out his handgun, but it fell to the deck with a clatter.

Suddenly, the guy whirled violently and broke Ren's hold. He shoved Ren hard, knocking him down. He leaped on top of Ren, his weight hitting Ren's chest. The man's gloved hands closed over his throat.

"Stop."

They both looked up. Halle stood there, with the man's dropped gun in her hands. She had it aimed right at his chest. And from the way she held it, it was clear she knew how to use it.

The attacker froze. Ren lunged up, jabbing a fist to the man's chest.

The guy stumbled. Ren hit him again, knocking him off balance. Then Ren lowered his shoulder and ran forward. He hit the guy hard, forcing him into the metal railing. The man cursed, but Ren kept up the pressure.

The intruder tipped over the railing and into the ocean.

"God," Halle said shakily.

Ren spun to the UUV. It was still resting in its storage container. He quickly clipped the crane hook to it. Then he activated the crane, lifting the drone into the water.

He heard shouts. He knew they'd hear the crane.

He glanced out at the horizon, noting the first glimmer of sunrise. They needed to get out of there. The drone hit the water with a splash.

"Ren?" Halle said. "What are you doing?"

"We need to leave." He pulled her down to the lowest part of the back deck. He flicked open a box and pulled out two wetsuits. He shoved one at her.

"But what about everyone else on the ship? We can't leave them."

"We can't help them against a team of armed intruders." With expert moves, he kicked off his shoes and pulled the wetsuit over his shorts and T-shirt. Halle did the same.

He shoved their shoes in his backpack and pulled her to the ship's edge. Waves slapped against the side of the vessel.

"Where are we going to go?" she asked.

"For a swim."

"Oh, God. We aren't near Hawaii yet. I can't swim that far."

"I can. And we'll have some help. We're going to take the UUV."

Voices were getting closer.

"Halle, I need you to get into the water and override the drone controls so we can control it manually. And you need to do it fast, before they see us."

She pressed a hand to her head, swallowed, then lifted her chin. "Okay."

He took her hand. "We jump together. Ready?"

"Not really."

"Go."

They dropped into the water. It was dark and the cold slapped him in the face. He heard Halle gasp.

He urged her toward the drone, and she gripped the fin. Ren circled his legs to tread water. She leaned over the UUV, tapping in the security code on the control panel. Water splashed into her face, but she stayed focused.

"There. I've switched it to manual controls."

"Hold on to the drone fin," he said. "As tightly as you can."

She gripped it and nodded.

Ren did too, pressing his body up against hers.

Then he reached over and activated the controls.

The drone zoomed forward, and he tightened his grip. As they sped away from the ship, he heard shouts and more gunfire.

He thought of his men on the ship, Captain Shroff, the research team. He closed his eyes.

A part of him hated abandoning them.

He opened his eyes. The best way to help them was to get to land, and get help.

OH, *God.*

Halle was terrified.

They were in the middle of the ocean at night.

She clung to the UUV as it pulled them through the water. Ren's body was pressed against hers.

Ren was with her.

That helped calm some of her fear.

She glanced back. She could see the lights of the *Atalanta*, and the shadows of people moving around on the deck.

The crew and her colleagues were being held hostage.

God. This couldn't be happening. "Ren..."

"It's okay, baby. I know we've got a long way to go, but we'll get to shore."

"Oahu?"

"No. The best I can tell, the closest island will be Molokai."

"Right." She felt a little shaky, and the water was cold.

"Just take a few deep breaths and stay calm."

Easier said than done, but she trusted Ren.

All of a sudden, she heard shouts coming from the ship behind them.

"Shit," Ren muttered.

"What?" Her pulse skittered.

"I think they're looking for us."

The sound of a motor revving caught her attention. She glanced back over her shoulder, and spotted a shadow detaching itself from the back of the ship. *Oh, no.* It was one of the zodiacs she'd seen stowed on the *Atalanta*.

From what she could see, there were several men inside it.

It was zooming away from the *Atalanta*.

"*Fuck.*" Ren touched the drone controls and the UUV stopped.

"What are you doing?"

"They're searching for us. I don't want them to detect us."

A flashlight beam appeared on the zodiac, sweeping across the water.

"Stay still and be quiet," Ren said. "Duck down as low as you can."

She dropped down in the water until only her eyes were visible over the top. There was a gentle swell, and they bobbed up and down with it.

Her fingers were so cold. Ren tightened his hold on her.

The zodiac was moving in a search pattern. A few minutes later, it came in their direction. She gripped Ren's arm. She could hear people talking.

"Is that Mandarin, or Cantonese?" she whispered.

"Yes," he said grimly.

The searchlight passed by, just a few feet away from them. She bit her lip. Her heart was beating so hard she was certain it would give them away.

The boat made some more zigzag movements, then finally turned away from them.

Halle blew out a ragged breath.

"Good job." Ren pressed a kiss to her head.

He sounded so calm. She realized this had to be the kind of dangerous situation he'd been in before.

He started the UUV again, and all she could hear was the near-silent hum of its engine.

"We're going to get to shore. I'll get you safe." He ruffled a hand through her hair, and his voice was as solid as a rock. "I promise you, Halle."

She dragged in a deep breath. "And we have to keep the fuel cell safe."

"We will."

She looked back at the ship. "I hope the others are all right."

"The best way to help them is to get to land and alert the authorities."

She nodded.

"Good girl." He hugged her. "So damn brave."

"I don't feel brave."

"You're holding up just fine. Now, hang on tight."

He touched the controls, and the UUV set off again.

All Halle could do was hold on, the occasional small wave splashing in her face. Grimly, she bit her lip, determined not to complain.

She wasn't sure how much time had passed, but as she stared ahead, pinpricks of light appeared in the distance. She blinked.

Wait, was that an island?

God, it still looked so far away. *But you're not alone, Halle.* She took another deep breath.

She and Ren could make it. And she wasn't going to do anything that would slow him down, or add to what he had to deal with. She was going to help him, not hinder him.

She wanted to keep him safe, too.

CHAPTER ELEVEN

The sun was rising, sending a glimmer of pink light along the horizon. Ren could see better now. The island was fully visible, just ahead of them—a white stretch of beach, and dense trees that filled the hillside.

The island of Molokai.

He knew the island had been formed by two shield volcanoes, and was the less touristy of all the Hawaiian islands.

Halle was silent, and when he glanced at her, he saw her face set in hard lines. He knew she was cold and tired, but she hadn't complained once.

Ren was wired with adrenaline. He wanted Halle out of the water and safe. Whoever attacked the *Atalanta* would be searching for them. The zodiac had kept up the search for several hours, and they'd had a few close calls.

They weren't out of the woods—or rather, the water—yet.

"We're nearly there," he said.

Halle gave him a weary nod.

As they got closer to land, the waves grew rougher. Ren used all his strength to aim them at the beach, and a second later, they caught a wave and washed into shore. The drone hit the sand.

Halle came up on her knees, then wearily pushed to her feet. "We made it."

"You did great."

"All I did was hang on." She set her shoulders back, determination on her face. "What now?"

So damn brave. He hugged her. "You did good, baby."

"I didn't want to slow us down." She clutched his arms. "I wanted to keep you safe."

Ren stilled. He'd been a SEAL, then in Ghost Ops. No one worried about him, or about him being safe. It was his job to worry about other people.

But as he stared into her blue eyes, he realized that she did.

"Oh, Ren." She cupped his cheeks. "Of course I want you safe." It was like she'd read his mind. "I want to take care of you."

Emotions tangled in his chest, and he cleared his throat. She might want him safe, but right now, it was his priority to protect her and the fuel cell.

"First thing we need to do is get the fuel cell out of the UUV."

She released a breath and glanced at the ocean. "They'll keep looking for us."

"Yes."

And he knew they were willing to kill for the fuel cell. He thought of poor Jack and squelched his anger.

I'll make them pay, buddy.

Halle dropped down beside the drone, and pressed the code into the fuel cell compartment. The door popped open, and she pulled the cell out. She passed it to him.

It was small but heavy.

He carefully put it in his backpack. "We need to hide the drone."

Together, they dragged the drone up the beach and into the vegetation. He laid some palm fronds over it. It wasn't ideal, but at a passing glance, it wouldn't attract any attention.

Using an extra palm frond, he cleaned up the tracks they'd left in the sand.

"What's the plan now?" she asked, scanning the trees.

"Hike to get help. Alert the authorities." He unzipped his wetsuit and tugged it down. "We'll stash these here as well."

She nodded. Soon, they both stood in their damp clothes with their shoes back on. Ren tucked the wetsuits under the UUV.

Halle tugged at the long sleeves on her T-shirt and looked at the forest. "Any idea how far we need to go?"

"Not exactly. My best guess is that we're at the eastern end of Molokai. It's mostly forests covering an extinct shield volcano. There are some roads and farms. We might come across someone who can help us."

"Are you sure the volcano is extinct?" She pulled a face. "After the night we've had, I'm expecting the worst. An erupting volcano would be right up there."

He tugged on her wet ponytail. "It's definitely extinct. It's probably going to be a long hike."

"Well, if you want to throw in a bike ride, we'll have a triathlon." She frowned. "That fuel cell is heavy."

"I've carried heavier packs during training and on missions." He took her hand. "Come on, Ariel."

They left the beach and headed into the forest.

The trees and vegetation were thick. Moss covered the tree trunks, and palm trees speared into the air. Lower down, ferns and other bushes covered the ground.

"Hiking in wet clothes is fun," Halle said.

"I know it sucks, but we'll dry out."

They trekked on, and as the sun got higher, he could see more of the forest around them. Birds squawked overhead.

He also saw that Halle was on the verge of exhaustion. She was soldiering on, but she needed some rest. They needed to find somewhere to take a break. Somewhere safe.

No one was getting their hands on Halle Bradshaw. He'd make sure of that.

HALLE TRUDGED THROUGH THE FOREST, focused on simply putting one foot in front of the other. At any other time, she'd think it was beautiful. She usually enjoyed hiking. But hiking after a wild, nighttime swim assisted by a classified drone, while escaping bad guys, not so much.

She swallowed. She was beyond tired, but she had to keep going.

Her worried mind kept thinking of Sammy and the others. She prayed they were okay. Fitz would be having a panic attack, and she worried Sammy or Ryan might try to fight back. Professor Davis would do his best to take care of them.

She glanced at Ren. He moved silently, each step sure and certain. He was also constantly scanning their surroundings.

Being with him eased some of the anxiety inside her that had manifested like a hard ball in her chest. He pushed himself so hard. With his work on the *Atalanta*, and now, taking care of her.

Who looked out for Ren?

She wanted to take care of him. Make him smile, laugh, relax.

She was so preoccupied with her thoughts, that the toe of her shoe caught on a thick vine, and she nearly tripped.

Throwing her arms out, she caught herself before she hit the ground. She huffed out a breath. *Focus, Halle.*

Ren glanced back at her. "You okay?"

She lifted a hand and pasted on a smile. "Fine."

They walked on, and before long, the temperature had risen dramatically. The sun beat down on them causing sweat to run down the back of her neck.

"I usually like hiking," she said.

He smiled. "Don't worry. We'll find somewhere to rest soon. I know you're tired."

"You must be tired too."

"I'm used to it."

"You're not in the military anymore, Ren. You're allowed to rest, and relax, and have fun. You don't need to push on all the time. You're allowed to live."

A frown crossed his face.

Halle bit her lip. "You told me that it wasn't just one thing that made you leave Ghost Ops. But I think there was something."

And just like that, she saw his face shut down.

She swallowed. "I know you think I'm too young and too innocent to handle whatever haunts you, Ren, but I'm not." She closed the distance between them. "I lived through my worst nightmare when I lost my mom. I can handle hearing yours, because I care about you."

He stared at her, his dark eyes churning with emotion. He shook his head and set off walking again.

Dammit, he was so stubborn. "Argh, Ren. Don't you just walk away from me." She stomped after him.

"We need to keep moving."

She grabbed his arm. "I have one more thing to say."

He stopped, his mouth a flat line.

"I'm not just attracted to your handsome face, and hot body. I don't just want sex. Or snuggles as we watch black-and-white TV shows. Or cotton candy. I mean, I love all those things, and I do want them." She took his hand in hers. "I want everything. I want the tough stuff as well. I want it all." She squeezed his fingers, then stepped back.

She'd let him chew on that.

Head held high, she headed up the track.

She sensed him following her, although he barely made a sound.

They hiked on a bit farther, scrambling over some downed trees and old stumps, when a familiar sound in the distance caught her ear. She straightened and cocked her head. "Is that—?"

He stepped up beside her and nodded. "A waterfall."

They made their way up a gentle slope, and the trees thinned out. Then, the waterfall came into view.

It was a long, narrow fall of water coming from up a steep cliffside. It fell into a large, shallow pool ringed by rocks and lush vegetation.

"It's beautiful." Halle moved to the pool and scooped up some water. She splashed it on her face and smiled.

Suddenly, another noise cut through the air.

Ren cursed. "Helicopter. We need to hide. *Now*."

He grabbed her arm and pulled her away from the water, and back into the dense vegetation. He found a thick clump of ferns. They ducked down, and Ren wrapped an arm around her. A helicopter thundered overhead.

Oh, God. She caught a glimpse of the navy-colored aircraft as it moved past. A second later, it circled again.

"Are they looking for us?" she said.

"Maybe. It could also be a helicopter tour." His arm tightened. "But even if that helo isn't carrying the people who took over the *Atalanta*, they will be looking for us."

She rested her head on his shoulder. "It sounded like they were Chinese, right?"

He nodded. "Maybe Chinese intelligence, or mercenaries."

"We can't let them get that fuel cell, Ren."

Finally, the sound of the helicopter died away. Halle's muscles relaxed.

Ren rose and pulled her up. "We need to keep moving."

They left the waterfall behind and trudged on, sticking close to the trees. Ren was much more tense and alert. About an hour had passed, when suddenly, he stopped.

"What is it?" she whispered.

"Look."

She followed his gaze. It took her a second, but then she made out the wooden cabin tucked in under the trees. Her heart leaped. Maybe there was someone who could help them? Maybe they had a telephone?

"Stay behind me," he ordered.

As they crept closer, her heart sank. The windows were broken. Vines and trees were growing into the empty cabin. It looked abandoned and overgrown.

"Think there's a working telephone?" she asked.

Ren smiled at her. "Don't get your hopes up. There are several abandoned places on Molokai. I read an article once about people trying to rezone land and sell it to developers, but the local government wouldn't allow it. There's even a resort that's fallen into ruin on the other end of the island."

She glanced around, and thought again of the pretty waterfall. "It would be a shame for this natural beauty to be replaced by condo towers and resorts."

He used his shoulder to push open the door.

Inside, the vines had taken over. The shack was

empty except for some overturned furniture. Ren righted a wooden stool and gestured for her to sit down.

"Let's take a short rest here."

He opened his backpack and handed her a granola bar. She chewed on it as she studied the cabin. She wondered who had lived here, and why they'd left.

Ren handed her a water bottle and she took a swig. He had a drink as well before he tucked the bottle away, and swung the bag back onto his back. "Time to keep going."

Halle heaved herself up. Her feet were aching, and she was tired, but she refused to complain.

They set off hiking again. Thankfully, there was no sign of the helicopter.

As they made their way through a dense patch of trees, some birds took flight from the branches. She marveled at the pretty colors among their fluttering wings and smiled. "My mom would've loved it here."

"You miss her."

Halle nodded. "All the time."

"I'm sorry you lost her."

"Me too, but loss is a part of life." She wrinkled her nose. "That's what I tell myself on the tougher days. Loving her and the love she gave me was worth the loss."

Ren's brow creased.

"I'm sorry you lost your friends," she said. "In the military."

"Yeah." He glanced away. "The hardest thing was knowing that some of them had wives, kids. Didn't seem fair that I made it home."

She whirled. "Don't tell me you think that because

you didn't have kids, or weren't married, that it would have been better if you'd died over there?"

"Well—"

Anger shot through her. "You have people who care about you, Lorenzo Santoro. People who love you."

He looked frozen. She slammed her hands against his chest.

"You've got yourself so locked up in there that you don't even realize. Look at me. Standing here in front of you." She shook her head. "I...care about you."

Now, he looked shocked. She would've laughed, if the expression on his face didn't hurt so much.

"Don't you dare say that I'm too young to know how I feel, or I'll hit you over the head with that damn fuel cell. I'll—"

He grabbed her, and hauled her close. "Halle."

The word was a harsh whisper.

"Yes, Ren. I care about you. I don't need you to be perfect, or have no baggage. We all have baggage. Just let me in."

With a groan, he kissed her.

His mouth was hard against hers, his tongue tracing her lip before plunging deep. She shivered, kissing him back with everything she felt.

He lowered them to their knees, and pressed his forehead to hers. "I don't deserve you."

"Stop saying that." She rubbed her thumb over his lips. "You absolutely deserve me. Everybody deserves someone."

He swallowed. "Everyone I've ever cared about left me."

Her heart squeezed. "Your father?"

"No, I never knew him. Losing my mom and abuela, so close together, was the worst."

"I'm sorry," she whispered. "They both died of cancer?"

He nodded. "Within a year of each other."

"They must have been so proud of the man you'd become."

"And my friends died. Over there in that hellhole." He paused. "And others."

"Tell me," she whispered.

"There was a little girl." He sucked in a breath. "Her name was Nasrin. She was nine. I was undercover, trying to ferret out the location of a group of Taliban who'd ambushed some of our soldiers." Ren paused. "A local man, Amir, helped me. Nasrin was his daughter. I..." He shook his head. "I fucked up, and the Taliban found out that Amir helped me. They took Nasrin. They hurt her, and killed her."

Halle sucked in a breath. She knew just how much the loss of a little girl's life would have destroyed him. "I'm sorry. I'm so sorry."

"I can still hear her screams. Her mother's wails. And Amir..." Ren sniffed. "They let him live, knowing she was gone. And I got safely back to base."

She wrapped her arms around him and held on tight. "It was a hard place. A terrible place."

"Fuck, caring for others hurts, Halle. Being responsible for them can hurt so much."

"But it can also bring joy and happiness. And it can

heal." She pressed a gentle kiss to his lips. "Let me show you."

He blew out a breath. "I don't know if I can, but I want to try."

She cupped his face, overwhelmed by emotion.

"Not just for me," he murmured. "For Nasrin. To honor her." He ran his thumbs along Halle's cheekbones. "But first, we need to get safe, and get this fuel cell where it needs to be."

She smoothed her hands down his chest, her fingers clenching on his shirt. "All right."

"Let's get moving."

CHAPTER TWELVE

As they moved up the hill, the vegetation thickened. Ren was damn glad the helicopter hadn't come back. His jaw tightened. There was no way to know who the occupants had been, but he hoped to hell it wasn't whoever was after the fuel cell.

That really didn't matter, though. He knew they'd be coming.

He needed to call for help. And they needed that help to get here fast.

He wouldn't have time to describe the situation to the local authorities. It would be best to call someone who'd get it straight away, and then immediately send in the cavalry.

He needed to call Sawyer and Vander.

As a deputy sheriff, Sawyer would know the local law enforcement. And Vander could contact the right people at the Navy.

Ren just needed to find a phone.

He glanced back, and realized that Halle had fallen

behind. She was moving slowly, her hands gripping tree trunks for support as she walked.

"Halle?" He hurried back down toward her.

"I am...okay," she wheezed.

But her face was pale, and her breathing was fast. He watched her chest rise and fall rapidly, and realized her breathing was labored.

She'd been fine earlier, even though she was tired.

"Sit," he urged her.

"Ren, we can't—" Her next breath sounded bad.

He eased her to the ground. "What's wrong?"

"Asthma..."

Shit. He sat behind her, and smoothed her hair off her sweaty forehead. "All right, just relax." His chest tightened. "Your inhaler's on the ship, right?"

She grimaced. "Right."

He looked around the jungle. Something here in the vegetation had to be triggering the attack. The stress of their situation wouldn't be helping, either.

Panic slipped through his veins like razor blades. If she had a full-blown attack right now, she could die.

"Take it easy," he said, trying to keep his tone calm. "Just relax and breathe."

She leaned back against him, and he stroked his hands down her arms.

Her eyes closed. "This is nice."

The minutes ticked by. Ren's jaw was clenched so tight it hurt. He hated this. He hated having an enemy he couldn't fight.

Her breathing eased a little, but he knew she needed medication or medical attention.

Resolve filled him.

Halle was the best damn thing in his life. He wasn't going to let her suffer.

He rose, then bent down to help her up. "You're getting a ride on my back for the next leg of this trip."

Her brow creased. "Ren, no—"

"I'm going to get help for you. Whatever it takes."

She stared at his face, obviously hearing the resolve in his voice. "You aren't going to let me walk?"

"Nope."

She sighed. "Fine, Mr. Stubborn."

He turned around and crouched down. She awkwardly climbed on. She wasn't moving with her usual grace.

He picked up the backpack, rose, and set off through the trees with Halle clinging to his back.

"I'm too heavy," she said.

"I'll carry you anywhere, Halle. Any time, any distance."

Her arms tightened around him. Her harsh breathing echoed in his ear. She needed a rescue inhaler.

And they were in the middle of the jungle, on one of the least populated islands in Hawaii.

He gritted his teeth. He *would* get her what she needed, one way or another. Whatever it took.

Before long, the land flattened out, and the trees thinned. A moment later, he stepped into a cleared area.

He paused and scrutinized the land around them.

The green grass was dotted with pretty purple flowers. It was cleared all the way down the hill.

"A farm?" she wheezed.

He spotted a long, wooden building in the distance, near a line of trees. There were also several small, wooden cabins dotting the land nearby.

He broke into a jog. "Hold on, Ariel."

As he got closer to the buildings, disappointment punched his gut. The structures looked like they weren't in use. There was no one around. His only hope rested on the fact that these buildings weren't in terrible disrepair, like the old cabin they'd found in the jungle.

He jogged up the steps of the main building, and spotted a chain and padlock on the double doors. He circled around the veranda. Halle was lolling on his back, and he thought her breathing sounded a little worse.

He tightened his hold on her legs. He wasn't losing her.

"It looks like a guest ranch," he said.

He found a side door, then used his elbow to smash the windowpane. He reached in and unlocked it.

He hurried inside. The door led to the kitchen. The room was empty, and had an air of disuse. He strode out into a dining room filled with wooden tables, the chairs all turned upside down and resting on top of the tables.

Continuing on, they entered a large, lobby area. There was a reception desk, and some low chairs—the fabric on them covered in colorful, hibiscus flowers.

He hurried to the desk and set Halle down on the floor. She leaned back against the desk, each breath labored and her face a frightening shade of gray.

Ren strode to the cabinets behind the reception desk and started yanking the doors open. It didn't look like this place had closed down that long ago. If they'd taken guests, they had to have some decent first aid supplies.

The shelves were filled with all kinds of things—towels, keys, books, candles, binders, office supplies.

"Come on." He yanked open the next cabinet, and finally saw something that made his pulse jump. A huge, red first aid kit.

Thank fuck. He grabbed it and swiveled. He knelt beside Halle, and opened the kit. He pulled items out, tearing through everything inside. He prayed there was a rescue inhaler in here.

Then he saw it. An inhaler.

He grabbed it. It was a rescue inhaler, and it hadn't expired.

He cupped Halle's cheek. "Halle. Here you go." He shook it, then held it to her lips.

With a shaky hand, she grabbed the inhaler and depressed the button. She inhaled, breathing slowly and deeply.

Ren pulled her onto his lap, holding her close. Finally, he heard the wheezing ease.

"I'm all right," she said quietly.

He pressed his face to her hair. *Thank God.*

"I'm all right because of you." She tangled her fingers with his.

"I'll always take care of you, baby. No matter what."

HALLE WAS FEELING MUCH BETTER, although still a little wobbly.

She watched Ren shove some things from the first aid kit into his backpack.

"Let's take a look around," he said. "If you're feeling up to it."

"I'm feeling all right, Ren." She'd reassured him numerous times that she was fine, but he clearly wasn't buying it quite yet.

They explored the rooms of the ranch lodge, with Ren sticking very close to her.

"Phones don't work." He smashed the phone back down onto the desk. He strode out of the office, his gaze running over her.

She lifted a folder with a laminated picture of the ranch on the front of it. "This was the Hill of Birds ranch. They grew all kinds of organic fruits and vegetables, and Hawaiian ʻawa root, and farmed honey. They also offered cabins for people to stay on the ranch. A rustic retreat, kind of thing."

"They must have gone bust."

She looked out the windows. The sun was heading for the horizon. It would get dark soon.

"Let's check out the cabins," he said. "You need to rest."

"We *both* need to rest."

They headed outside. Ren picked the most distant cabin, that lay close to the tree line. He broke another window to get in.

Halle stepped inside. "This is lovely."

The walls were painted white, and the floor was a rich, red wood. A large bed was situated to take in the beautiful, lush view out the large, picture window. In the distance, the ocean glittered.

The bed had been stripped, but when she opened the nearby cupboard, she found some folded blankets.

Ren came out of the bathroom. "The water works, and it's warm."

Her brows rose. "How?"

"I did see a solar-panel system back near the main lodge. There's no electricity though." He flicked a light switch off and on. Then he opened some drawers and found some candles. "But these will do the job." Then he went and pulled all the curtains closed. "I don't want anyone to notice we're here." He eyed her. "I think you should take a bath next, while I see if I can find us some food."

A bath sounded like heaven, and she nearly trembled at the idea. She watched him head into the bathroom and then heard water running.

She followed him, and her mouth dropped open. There was a gorgeous free-standing tub in front of another window. He'd already closed the blinds, and was lighting a candle.

He turned to face her. "You'll be okay while I'm gone?"

She nodded. "Don't be long, though."

He ran a thumb across her cheek. "I won't. I'm going to head back to the lodge and check out the main kitchen."

Then he was gone. She nudged the curtain aside, watching him disappear into the growing darkness like a ghost.

When the bath was full, Halle stripped off her clothes and climbed in. The warm water made her whimper. She leaned back, the water lapping at her skin, but when she tried to relax, she was too restless.

She didn't like Ren being out of sight.

"He's a badass. He'll be back." She closed her eyes.

"Hey, sleeping beauty."

Her eyes popped open, and she saw Ren kneeling beside the tub. The candlelight flickered over his handsome face.

"Hi." She blinked. "God, did I fall asleep?"

"Yes," he said, amused. "Time to get out before you drown."

She nodded. "Any luck with food?"

"I found a few canned goods, and things. I'll set it out." He disappeared out of the bathroom.

Halle dried off, and saw that he'd left her a thick, white robe. She pulled it on.

Okay, they weren't safe yet, but they were safe-ish. She tugged on the lapels of the robe. She needed to recharge while she had the chance, because tomorrow, they'd be hiking again to find help.

When she came out of the bathroom, Ren had set out a feast of sorts. There were crackers, jarred pickles, beef jerky, and a large variety of dried fruit. She guessed the ranch had done a lot of the dehydrating themselves.

"Well, this is gourmet," she said with a smile.

He smiled back. "I've eaten a lot worse."

She sat on the bed beside him, and picked up some slices of dried banana. They ate in companionable silence, and she was grateful they had somewhere warm and comfortable to rest.

"What's our plan?" she asked. She had no doubt he'd have one.

"We'll rest here tonight. Tomorrow, we'll set off first thing to find a road. See if we can flag someone down to take us to the nearest town."

She chewed on a cracker, and soon her eyes started to droop.

Ren took the rest of the food and set it on the nightstand. Then he gently eased her back onto the pillows.

"It's too early to sleep," she said, voice slurred.

"We did get woken up in the middle of the night, then had to swim and hike. You're exhausted." He smoothed a hand over her hair. "Time to rest."

She grabbed his hand. "I'm glad you're with me, Ren. I'm glad we're together."

"Me too, baby. Sleep. I'll be here." He kissed her forehead.

Halle drifted off to sleep. As she did, she heard him murmur again.

"I won't let them touch you. Whatever it takes."

CHAPTER THIRTEEN

Ren sat in a chair by the window. He kept checking outside. Night had fallen, and Halle had been asleep for a few hours.

She was curled up on the bed, like a sleeping princess.

He blew out a breath and watched her. He'd lit a candle beside the bed, and the warm light made her skin glow. He'd been watching the steady rise and fall of her chest for a while. During her asthma attack, he'd been terrified, watching her struggling to breathe.

He could fight the bad guys, but he couldn't fight off a damn asthma attack.

He gripped his thighs. He'd felt helpless.

Caring for someone, loving someone, left you so vulnerable. His chest tightened. It was a part of the reason he'd avoided getting too close to anyone. It was why being on the *Atalanta* suited him. Losing his mom and grandmother had hurt so much. They'd been gentle souls. The softness in his life.

Then they'd been gone. Stolen away by another disease he couldn't fight.

And there was one other reason he'd avoided Halle.

He loved her.

Jesus. He loved her. Not as a family friend, or the daughter of a man he respected.

He was in love with her. With her smart mind, her kind soul, her freckles, her sweet body.

On the bed, Halle stirred and sat up. When she saw him, she smiled.

There.

That, right there, was worth everything.

"Is everything all right?" she asked.

He gave her a brief nod.

She shifted again and the robe gaped, giving him a glimpse of her naked breasts. His cock twitched.

"We're safe here?" she asked.

He nodded again

"Good." She held out a hand. "Come here, Ren."

He quivered. "Why?"

"Because you're mine. And I want you to touch me."

Her words ignited flames inside him.

"I want you to touch me." She shifted her shoulders and nudged the robe off. It fell to her waist. He stared hungrily at her bare breasts. The full curves, her already tight nipples.

"I want you to kiss me. I want you to spank me again, and put your fingers inside me."

He groaned. His muscles were tense, and he felt ready to snap.

"I want you inside me, Ren. I want to feel you

moving inside me." She licked her lips. "I need to know what that feels like."

His cock was leaking in his damn pants. A growl escaped him—wild, vicious, needy.

He surged up and strode to the bed. He yanked her to him, and slammed his mouth down on hers.

He knew he was being too rough, but she made a needy sound and desperately kissed him back. He slid his hand into her hair and forced himself to slow down a little. To savor.

Her plush mouth opened for him, the taste of her hitting him hard. So damn sweet.

Then she'd rocked against him, trying to press closer.

"Please, Ren," she said against his lips. "I'm yours, and you're mine."

"Yes, you're mine. All mine." He pushed her down, and shoved the rest of the robe off her body. He cupped her breasts, squeezed, and enjoyed the weight filling his palms. He pushed them together. Fuck, he loved seeing his big, tanned hands against her golden skin.

She moaned. "That feels good."

He rubbed his thumbs over her hard nipples. She arched her body, like an offering.

Ren slid his hands down her sides, then drew traces over her belly with his fingertips. "You look like a goddess, Halle."

"I'm not. I'm just a woman, who really, really wants you."

Then he stroked between her legs.

Her lips parted, her cheeks flushed in the candlelight.

"So damn gorgeous." He leaned over and put his

mouth on her breast. As he sucked and tugged at her nipple, he slid a finger inside her.

She moaned for him.

"You're tight, baby. Need to get you ready."

She nodded. He reached for one of her hands and pulled it down between her thighs. Holding her fingers with his, they stroked her together.

She let out a soft sigh.

"You've touched yourself before?" he asked.

She nodded. "And thought of you. Imagined your fingers inside me. Your cock inside me."

Hell, she was killing him. "Slide your finger inside your pussy, Halle."

"Oh..." She blew out a breath.

Ren slid a finger in beside hers, and let his thumb brush her clit. She whimpered.

"Push in and out, nice and slow." He helped her. "That's the way. You'll take my cock like that soon."

"Yes, yes."

He felt a hand tug on his pants. He reached out and helped her to open them. Then he straightened, and pulled his T-shirt off. "Don't stop touching yourself."

She was busy ripping his pants open, and a second later, she got his cock free. She dragged her free hand over it, and played with the slick pre-come at the head. Her other hand stayed buried between her legs.

He groaned and thrust against her palm.

"A part of me wants to go slow," he growled. "To tease you, take my time." He shook his head. "But I can't. Not this time."

"I want you inside me, Ren. Now. I don't want slow. I want *you*."

His chest heaved. "I don't have a condom."

She bit her lip. "Good."

He groaned again.

"I'm on birth control," she told him.

"And I'm clean. It's been a long time."

"How long?"

He felt stripped bare. "Since I kissed you on your birthday."

Her eyes went wide. "*Ren.*"

He dipped his fingers between her legs again, and stroked her slick flesh. He needed to make sure she was ready for him. He loved the way she gasped and writhed under his touch.

"I can't wait to feel your tight, little pussy squeezing my cock."

Her hips rocked into his touch.

"I've imagined it so many times." He kicked the rest of his clothes off and covered her body with his. He shoved her thighs apart and lined his cock up. He pressed forward, until just the fat head of his cock was inside her.

Their moans mingled.

"This might hurt," he said.

"I know. I don't care."

He sank in another inch. She was tight as hell, and he sucked in a quick breath. He wanted to make it good for her.

"You can take me, baby." He pushed forward another inch. "Just a little. I'll take it easy."

Her hands clenched on him. "It feels good, but I'm so full. You're so big."

His muscles strained. He wanted to slam into her. "You can take me." He closed his eyes, felt on the verge of coming. He fought it back.

When he opened his eyes, he saw her eyes were glazed over. She nodded at him. "Take me, Lorenzo. Give me all of you."

With a groan, he thrust inside her.

She cried out, sucking in fast breaths as she adjusted to his size.

"Halle?" His voice was uneven. He was about to lose his mind.

"Don't stop," she whispered.

"Couldn't even if I wanted to."

She ran her hands down his back. "You're so deep inside me."

"Yeah, baby. You're stuffed full of me."

Her fingers moved lower and gripped his ass. "Fuck me, Ren."

"*Halle.*" Sensation and pure instinct took over. The need to mate and claim. He drove into her, over and over again.

HALLE CRIED out at the way Ren filled her, moved inside her.

She loved the way he stretched her.

At first, it had felt strange, foreign. But the pressure had eased, and now she felt the pleasure.

It was just her and Ren.

Joined.

She forced her eyes open and met his gaze. Desire and need blazed through her, and she saw it echoed on his handsome face.

"Don't stop," she panted. "Don't ever stop."

"Halle, baby." He pounded into her now, and she dug her fingers into his hard muscles.

The way he filled her hit places she hadn't known existed. She felt all her muscles tensing, heat building.

He slowed his thrusts and leaned back. He looked down her body, dark desire on his face. "Look at you. Look at you take me." He thrust forward. "Look how deep I am inside you."

His words made her belly clench. She looked down and caught a glimpse of his thick, wet cock moving inside her.

She curled her toes and she clutched at him. She clawed at his back. "Oh, God. I..."

There was too much feeling, too much pleasure.

He groaned. "I feel you clamping down on me. You want me to come? Want me to fill you up?"

She made a desperate sound.

He groaned and slid one hand into her hair, fisting tight.

Halle's orgasm hit in a blinding rush. She cried out his name, her vision flaring white. She felt like the pleasure was being wrenched from her soul.

Ren held her harder, fucked her harder and wilder.

"Halle, Christ, I—" His deep groan echoed in her ears.

She felt him start coming too, and it prolonged her own release. She felt him pulse inside her. Holding on tight to his broad shoulders, she watched him come. He was so beautiful. She rode through the waves of pleasure, her cries filling the room.

Finally, he collapsed on the bed beside her, and pressed his face to her neck.

Halle couldn't talk. She felt...changed. Like she'd been pulled apart and put back together. All she could do was try and even out her breathing.

"Well, now I know why people are crazy about sex," she said breathlessly.

He lifted his head, his dark hair tousled. "That wasn't sex."

She blinked. "Oh?"

"That was special." He ran a thumb over her lips. "It's not always like that, Halle. It's never been like that for me before." He rubbed her lip again. "You're a miracle, you know that?"

She flushed.

He tapped her nose. "Wait here, and don't move."

He rose and headed for the bathroom.

Her gaze fell to his ass as he walked. She'd never had a thing for asses before, never got the attraction.

She bit her lip. Now she did.

Wait, were those scratches on his back? She blushed. Oh, crap, she'd done that. She wasn't sure if she should feel bad or proud.

He returned to the bed with a warm washcloth. She flushed as he nudged her thighs apart, and cleaned her. It was so intimate.

"Sore?" he asked.

She shook her head.

"You probably will be later."

"It was worth it."

He rose again to get rid of the cloth. When he returned, she noticed his cock wasn't fully soft.

Without thinking, she reached out and stroked it. He froze, and it hardened in her hand.

"Mmm."

He closed his eyes for a second. "It gets like that around you."

She kept stroking, exploring him. "There are more things I've always wanted to try."

His face looked strained. "You should rest."

She pulled him closer. "*After.*"

He released a shuddering breath. "What do you want to try?"

For a second, she felt a rush of shyness. But this was Ren and she trusted him. *Just be yourself.*

Every fantasy she'd had about Ren rushed through her head. Where to start?

"I want to keep stroking you until you..." She pressed the other hand to her breasts. "I...want you to come on me."

His brown gaze flared. "*Fuck.*"

The raw desire in his voice made her squirm. She saw what she did to him, and it made her feel sexy.

"And I want to be on top," she said.

"You'll be too sore to take me again."

"We'll see." She pulled him closer, then licked the head of his cock. She was rewarded with a low groan.

She'd given a couple of blow jobs in college, and hadn't found them much fun. She enjoyed it with Ren.

His thumb slid across her jaw. "You want to suck my cock, Halle?"

"Yes." She wanted him in her mouth again. Badly. She pressed her thighs together, and ran her hand up the length of his cock. Like the rest of him, it was long and hard.

Tilting her head back, she looked up at him.

"Damn you and your big, innocent eyes." He gripped his cock and angled it toward her mouth. "Open up, baby."

She opened her mouth, and he pushed past her lips. She moaned, and sucked him deep. He let out a low growl.

Something told her that she was going to enjoy this very much.

CHAPTER FOURTEEN

Ren drove into Halle from behind.

She moaned. He clamped his hands on her hips, holding her still for his thrusts.

She panted softly, her hands twisting into the covers. He felt every sound she made in his balls. She tilted her head, and he saw the curve of her jaw, her parted lips, and her hooded eyes. With every thrust, her breasts bounced.

His little, no-longer-a-virgin temptress had let him come on her pretty breasts. Then she'd coaxed him into sliding inside her again.

"More," she murmured. "*Deeper*."

Ren covered her back with his body, sliding a hand into her hair. He tugged until her head tilted back. He drove inside her.

Not once had she been afraid to show him what she was feeling, or what she wanted.

"Who's inside you, Halle?"

"You are, Ren."

He'd wanted to be gentle. Knew she'd be tender. But the way she begged him to go deeper, the way he felt her rippling around him, he couldn't stop or go slower.

He reached under her body, between her thighs, and felt where she was taking him. Her delicate skin that had never taken a man before him was stretched tight around his cock. He found her swollen clit and stroked.

She cried out.

He felt her pussy ripple around him. With a groan, he plunged fast and deep.

She came with a sharp cry. Damn, he'd never get enough of the feel of her coming. The sounds she made, the way she felt.

Fingers clamping on the hips, he buried himself deep and came inside her.

Fuck.

His vision grayed and he held her tight as the pleasure roared through him. He arched his back, and savored the connection between them.

When the searing intensity finally subsided, he dropped onto the bed beside her, and she turned and curled into him. That small, trusting move tugged at his heart. He wrapped an arm around her.

"Told you that I wasn't too sore," she said.

He ran his hand down her back. "Baby, I'm not going to complain." He pulled the covers over them.

He'd snuggle with her for a few minutes, until she fell asleep. But he wasn't planning to sleep tonight. He needed to keep watch. Needed to keep her safe.

She nuzzled her face against his chest. "I *really* like sex."

He kissed the top of her head. "I'm glad, baby." He could tell from her slurred voice that she was sleepy. He breathed in the scent of her clean hair. "Sleep now, Ariel."

"Okay, Ren. Night." Her eyelids closed.

"Night, baby."

He held her as she snuggled deeper. A few minutes later, he felt her breathing even out and her body relax as she fell asleep.

Emotions he'd been holding back for a long time stormed through him. *Damn.* He looked at the candlelight flickering on the ceiling, his arm holding Halle tightening.

He felt like the lock on his heart, on the place where he kept his darkest memories, had cracked.

She made a sound, and he relaxed his hold.

But deep down, Ren knew he'd never be able to let her go.

REN LISTENED to Halle's soft breathing.

He'd touched every part of her. Claimed her as his.

His hand curled. He would never be good enough for her, but she made him believe he could be.

He vowed to do whatever he could to make her happy.

You're mine now, Halle Bradshaw.

She'd delighted in every second where he'd lost himself in her.

No, that wasn't right. He was realizing that he'd actually found himself in her. When he was with her—whether holding her, listening to her talk, or inside her—everything noisy inside him went quiet.

Everything felt right.

Despite her complaints, he'd woken her long enough to get dressed before she'd fallen back asleep. At first light, they had to go.

He leaned his head back against the wall. While he'd preferred sleeping with her wrapped in his arms, he was fine sitting there in the quiet darkness, keeping watch over her.

His backpack rested by his leg, and he glared at the dark shadow of it. That damn fuel cell had caused a lot of trouble. Had put Halle at risk.

When he found out who'd betrayed them, he'd make sure they paid.

He heard a sound outside.

Ren tensed. Maybe it was an animal?

He pushed the curtain aside the smallest inch. It was dark outside, but moonlight washed over the ranch. He scanned the other cabins, and didn't see anything.

He kept watching.

There.

A shadow moved by one of the other cabins. He sucked in a breath.

Another one. Near the lodge.

A team in black was moving through the ranch.

Fuck.

He slowly settled the curtain back into place. He moved to the bed and shook Halle awake.

"Halle." He kept his voice low.

She jolted. "Ren?"

"Shh. We have company. Get your shoes on."

He couldn't see her face, but he heard a sharp breath.

"Okay." She pulled her shoes on and then ripped the blanket off the bed. She shoved it in the cupboard. "So, if someone checks, it won't look like we were here."

"Good thinking."

Ren pulled his backpack on and double checked his handgun. They moved to the back door, and he cracked it open, checking that there was no one outside. He tapped Halle's arm and crept outside, pulling her with him. The night air was cool.

He pressed his mouth to her ear. "Stay right behind me." Then he pressed a quick kiss to the side of her head.

He waited a beat, and made sure there were no signs of the intruders. Then he tugged her behind him, heading straight for the trees.

Halle couldn't move silently. Every noisy footfall, every snapped twig, made him wince. He shook his head. She was doing the best she could.

Finally, they made it to the trees. He pointed ahead, and she nodded.

They moved deeper into the forest. They needed to put as much ground as possible between them and their pursuers.

Without warning, a dark shape rounded a tree. The man was cradling an assault rifle. When he saw them, his eyes widened behind his mask.

Fuck.

Ren leaped at the man.

They crashed to the ground. Ren wrestled for the

weapon, and yanked it out of the man's hands. He pinned the attacker to the ground.

The man jerked up, and knocked Ren off balance.

They grappled, and rolled across the ground, both grunting. The guy was smaller than Ren, but strong.

But Ren was better trained.

And he had more to fight for.

He rolled, and got the guy in a headlock. The man tried to twist free, but Ren held on tight, pulling him backward. Then he got a firm hold on the guy's jaw, and twisted.

There was a dull crack.

The man's body went slack. Ren knew he couldn't let the man warn his team. He dropped the body and rose.

"Ren?"

Halle was watching him, her hands twisted together.

Shit, she'd watched him kill a man. Again.

Was she afraid of him?

"It's okay." Grimly, he dragged the body into the bushes. Then he crouched and pulled the man's mask off.

He was Asian. Ren released a breath, and straightened. "We have to move. Fast."

She came straight to him and wrapped her arms around him. "Then let's move. Thank you. For protecting me."

Something tight inside him eased. She wasn't afraid of him. He cupped her jaw. "Always."

They heard noises in the distance. He took her hand and pulled her deeper into the trees.

HALLE RAN THROUGH THE FOREST, desperately trying not to trip.

She could barely see. Occasional shafts of moonlight filtered through the trees and helped, but unlike Ren, who could clearly see in the dark, she felt like she was stumbling around blind.

She'd gone from a warm bed, and memories of making love with Ren, to running for her life.

Focus, Halle. They had to keep the fuel cell safe.

They had to find help.

The terrain got hillier, and her thighs were burning. She knew she was slowing Ren down.

He reached out and grabbed her arm. "You okay?"

She lifted her chin. "Yes."

Shouts echoed in the distance, and they both looked back. Down the hill, she saw beams of flashlights shining around.

"*Dammit,*" Ren said. "They must have found the guy I took down. Come on. We need to move faster."

She gripped his hand and followed him. She wasn't sure she had any faster in her.

They kept jogging, twisting through the trees. When she looked back, her body tightened. God, the lights were getting closer.

"Ren, they're coming this way."

"They must be tracking us. They must have someone who can read our trail." His tone was as hard as steel. "Come on, we need to hide." He turned sharp left, and moved down a steep slope.

She skidded behind him.

At the bottom was a fallen tree. In the murky light,

she saw that the bulk of the large log was covered in moss, and ferns surrounded it.

Then Ren cursed under his breath. "Careful." He grabbed her shoulders. "Don't move that way. There's the mouth of a cave there, and it looks like it's deep."

"It's probably an old lava tube," she said. "Parts of the Hawaiian Islands are riddled with them. The lava in active volcanoes forms natural conduits. When the lava tube empties, it leaves behind a cave."

He pulled her down behind the log. "Stay here."

She tucked in close to the log. "Where are you going?"

"I need to hide our tracks so these bastards can't find us." He disappeared into the shadows.

With him gone, her fear intensified. Halle pulled her legs to her chest.

Thankfully, it was only moments before he was back. He sat down beside her.

But before she could relax, she heard voices. There were definitely speaking in an Asian dialect, and getting closer.

Go past. She willed them in her head. *Please, go past.*

The voices drifted away. She looked at Ren. There was more light now, and she knew it wouldn't be much longer before the sun rose.

It would make it harder for them to hide, or slip away unnoticed.

Ren held a finger to his lips.

With a nod, she leaned into him.

It would be fine. Ren was with her. They'd get to the authorities, and then this nightmare would be over.

Finally, Ren rose cautiously. Halle stood and dusted off her butt.

An attacker dropped from a tree.

She gasped and pressed a hand to her mouth. She stumbled backward.

The man slammed into Ren, and they grappled. They shoved at each other, trading several punches.

Ren staggered back and fell against the log. The attacker drew a knife from his belt, the blade glinting in the early morning light.

No. Her heart lodged in her throat.

He swiped at Ren. Ren dodged, and caught the man's arm. He then rammed his knee into the man's stomach. They whirled, and the man moved fast, like a striking snake. He slashed at Ren again.

She heard Ren grunt. *God, was he hit?* Her pulse spiked.

Then Ren grabbed the man, and slammed him back against the fallen log. He pinned the attacker in place, then rammed his head forward, headbutting the man.

The attacker slumped, looking dazed. Ren landed a punch directly to his face.

But suddenly, the man rolled sideways. He spun to his feet, leaped into the air, and landed a kick to Ren's jaw. She watched his head snap back.

A choked cry escaped her. She had to help him.

She moved her hand around the ground and her fingers closed over a large stick.

The attacker and Ren were struggling and straining against each other. The attacker kicked again, knocking

Ren off his feet. He fell to the ground, and the man reared above him, lifting the knife.

Halle ran forward and swung the stick like a bat. She cracked the man in the face.

He flew backward, and landed flat on his back in some plants. He didn't get up.

"Is he dead?" She wasn't sure if she was happy or horrified.

Ren rose and checked the man. "Out cold." He quickly pulled the laces off the man's boots, then tied his hands and ankles. Next, he yanked off the man's mask, and fashioned a makeshift gag. "We need to go a different way. *Now.*"

She nodded. They started down another path, moving through the dense trees. She slapped ferns and large leaves out of her way. The sky was growing paler, and she could see more now. She noted several cave openings as they carefully passed by them.

God, one wrong step, and they could have tumbled inside the lava tubes.

The ground got steeper. Her shoes slipped. "*Ren.*" Suddenly, she lost her balance, arms windmilling. Then she tumbled down the slope.

She crashed through some bushes and heard Ren curse. She tumbled over and over again. Something stabbed into her side and then something hard slapped against her thigh.

Finally, she rolled to a stop, flopping onto her belly. *Ow*. Wincing, she lay there panting, sprawled on the ground.

Ren skidded to a stop beside her. "Halle, are you all right?"

He helped her up.

"I'm fine." Her clothes were smeared with dirt and leaves. "Sorry, I wasn't watching—" She stepped back.

"Halle, no."

She realized there was nothing under her foot.

"Ren!" She grabbed at him.

He lunged forward, but his weight overbalanced her. It tumbled them both into the cave opening neither of them had noticed.

Suddenly, they were falling. Ren wrapped his arms around her, and a scream caught in her throat.

A second later, they hit the ground.

Pain was like a sharp slap to the face.

Beside her, Ren groaned. Pain throbbed through Halle's chest, and she grimaced. She was winded, struggling to breathe. She rolled toward him.

"Ren?" she croaked.

"I'm...okay." He coughed.

Halle lay on the floor of the cave and looked up. A faint light glowed high overhead from where they'd fallen.

Oh, hell.

They were stuck at the bottom of a lava tube cave.

CHAPTER FIFTEEN

Ren swallowed a groan, and sat up. Everything ached.

"Halle?"

"I'm all right." She moved her shoulders and winced. "But it's going to hurt tomorrow."

He leaned over and cupped her cheek.

Then she looked down, and her blue eyes went wide. "Ren, you're bleeding." Panicked, she tugged at his shirt. "There's blood."

"It's okay. I just got nicked by the knife."

She sucked in a sharp breath. "You mean stabbed."

"No, nicked."

"Just like a man." She huffed out a breath. "Dad does the same thing. Downplays all his injuries."

She yanked Ren's shirt up and uncovered the wound. The cut was bleeding sluggishly.

He didn't have the heart to tell her he'd been both stabbed and cut before, or that this didn't even rate a mention.

She grabbed the backpack, and tore it open. She found the medical supplies he'd stuffed in there from the lodge. She ripped open a packet, and carefully pressed a bandage over his skin.

Then she leaned against him.

He hugged her close. "It's going to be okay."

She sniffed.

"You're not hurt? You didn't break anything in the fall?" He patted down her arms and sides.

"I have a few bumps and scrapes, but I'm fine."

He pushed her hair back from her face. It was loose and tangled. She looked so young.

But when her gaze met his, it was steady, gleaming with that intelligence of hers.

"Now what?" she asked.

"We climb out of here."

She groaned. "I figured you were going to say that."

Ren rose and studied the rock wall. He pointed. "This part here isn't as steep. There are a few good handholds."

She nodded, gnawing on her lip as she studied the wall.

That's when Ren heard noises above..

He moved fast, and pushed Halle against the wall. He pressed a finger to his lips.

It was their attackers. They were speaking Mandarin. Ren listened as they moved around above the cave entrance. Finally, the sounds faded.

Beside him, Halle released a shaky breath. "They're gone."

Ren nodded. He hoped they stayed gone. "I'll climb up first, and find the best path."

"Be careful."

He pulled the backpack on, then faced the wall. He reached up, and ran his hands over the rock. He got a good grip, and pushed himself up. Then he started climbing.

He moved slowly and steadily. His cut tugged a few times, and he had several other aches that he tried to ignore. Sore muscles were nothing. Thankfully, he hadn't broken anything in the fall. It was a damn miracle.

He had to get Halle out. That was the most important thing.

He moved past the halfway point. At a trickier spot, he paused, searching for his next handhold. Reaching up, he moved to haul his weight upward when his boot slipped.

"*Ren*," Halle cried.

He caught himself, hugging the rock. "I'm all right."

He took a second to catch his breath, then kept climbing. He was getting closer to the top. He gritted his teeth. He wasn't stopping.

Reach up, pull, climb.

Reach up, pull, climb.

Finally, his hands curved over the top of the cave entrance, and he hauled himself up. He pushed several fern fronds out of the way.

"Made it," he called down.

"Thank God."

He carefully poked his head out, and checked the vicinity. There was no one around.

He turned and laid flat on his stomach. He stuck his head over the edge. "Okay, Halle. Follow the path that I used."

"Ren... I'm not sure I can do it."

"You can do it, Halle. I'm pretty sure you can do anything."

She dragged in a deep breath, then pressed her hands to the wall. She started climbing, but she was moving very slowly and cautiously. He understood how scary this was for her.

She was about a third of the way up when she stopped to catch her breath.

"You're doing great, baby."

"I appreciate the lie." She reached up and kept climbing.

Ren watched her getting closer. Every time she glanced up at him, he could make out all the angles of her pretty face.

She smiled up at him and that's when her hand slipped. She yelped.

Ren's heart leaped into his throat. "Halle!"

She slid a foot or so down the wall, then caught herself. She clung to the rock, shivering.

"Take your time, baby. You've got this."

"I'm not sure I do."

"You do, Halle Bradshaw. You didn't give up on me. You forced me to face how I feel about you. You wouldn't let me keep running. You wouldn't let me keep lying to myself."

Her blue gaze locked on his. "How do you feel about me?"

"Come up here and I'll tell you."

"You're evil, Ren Santoro." She reached up and kept climbing. Her movements were even slower now, deliberate. She checked every handhold before she put weight on it. He could see her arms were shaking from the strain.

She inched closer to the top. He could almost touch her.

Her foot slipped.

Ren reached out and grabbed her wrist.

"*God.*" She pressed her feet to the rock, but her other arm was hanging out over the cave.

"I've got you."

She pressed her hand to the wall again, and he pulled her up. A second later, she was in his arms.

She burrowed into him.

"I knew you'd make it." He pressed a kiss to her hair.

"You gave me good incentive." She sounded a little shaky.

He covered her mouth with his and kissed her. Then he peppered kisses over her cheeks, her eyelids, her forehead. "Halle, God, I—"

That's when they heard voices. Getting closer.

They both stiffened.

"*Fuck.* Relentless bastards." He pulled her to her feet, then he pointed to the trees. "We have to go."

They ran into the trees. He heard shouts, and knew that their pursuers had heard them.

They dodged through several trees, but he heard voices ahead of them, too, and swiveled left.

Damn, there were too many of them.

Ren pulled the backpack off his back. He saw a tree

ahead with a hollow in the center of its trunk. As he jogged past, he stashed the backpack in the hollow.

They continued on, but as they slapped some fern fronds out of the way, he saw movement.

Suddenly, they were surrounded.

Halle stumbled to a halt and gasped. Ren stopped behind her, his hand curling into a fist.

Four men in black masks formed a semi-circle in front of them. They all had weapons aimed at him and Halle.

NO. *No. No.*

Halle looked around, fear choking her.

The men had guns aimed mostly on Ren, but one was aiming his weapon at her.

Ren raised his hands in the air, and Halle did the same.

One of the men circled around them, and then he kicked Ren's legs out from under him. Ren dropped heavily to his knees.

Then Halle felt a gun barrel jab her in the lower back.

"Down," the man bit out in slightly accented English.

She lowered slowly to the ground.

The man roughly searched them. She watched him take Ren's handguns.

Another man stepped forward. Something about the way he held himself made her think he was the boss.

"Where is the fuel cell?"

Ren just glared at him.

The man lifted a boot and kicked Ren viciously in the chest. Halle cried out.

"Where is it?" the man repeated. "Give it to us, and we'll let you live."

Ren made a harsh sound. "No, you won't."

The men all turned and talked to each other in Mandarin. Halle tried to calm her rapid breathing.

Then the leader nodded.

Suddenly, she was dragged up by her hair. She cried out. Ren lunged for her, but one of the other men hit him with the butt of his rifle.

Then a second man kicked Ren in the back.

"Stop it!" she screamed.

She watched Ren curl over as they attacked him.

The man behind her was holding her tight. She tried to pull free, but he jerked her back roughly.

She tried to ram her elbow back into his stomach, but his hand snapped out and he hit her in the face.

Dazed, she glanced down at Ren. Two of the men were holding him back. He was fighting to reach her, his face fierce.

She knew he'd try to save her. And they'd kill them.

Swallowing the jagged lump in her throat, she forced herself to relax.

It was hard when she was so afraid. Afraid for herself, and for Ren.

She heard a *snick*. Then a knife was held up in front of her face. Her pulse took off like a racehorse.

"Tell us the location of the fuel cell," the leader said again. "Or we'll start cutting her."

The blade pressed to her cheek. She couldn't stop her sharp exhalation.

On the ground, Ren's jaw worked.

"Don't say anything," she told him.

The man holding her moved his wrist, and she felt a quick sting on her cheek.

She gasped and felt blood slide down her skin.

Ren growled.

Then her captor moved the knife to her throat, and she stilled. He pressed the tip against her skin.

Her chest was rising and falling quickly. She locked her gaze on Ren's brown eyes.

"Perhaps we'll cut her throat next," the man said. "Or..." He nodded at the man holding her.

The knife moved to her ear.

"I will give you a nice souvenir."

"Leave her alone," Ren gritted out. "I swear I will kill you. I'll kill you all."

The man laughed, then straightened. "Where is the fuel cell?"

The knife pressed deeper against her ear and she bit her tongue. She wasn't going to scream.

"It's back there." Ren jerked his head toward the tree. "The tree with the hole in the trunk. There's a backpack in there."

"Ren, no!" she cried.

"Your life is more important."

But they'd kill them anyway. She really didn't want to die. She wanted to live. She wanted a life with Ren.

One of the men went back down the path. A moment

later he returned with the backpack. He unzipped it and tipped the contents on to the ground in front of them.

There was a dull thud as the fuel cell hit the dirt.

The men all spoke excitedly. One of them lifted the fuel cell.

"You two stay back here," the leader ordered two of his men. Even with a mask on, she could tell he was smiling. "Kill them."

Halle's chest locked tight. *No.* The asshole had spoken in English so they could understand, and be afraid.

"Meet us at the vehicle when you're done." The man spun and stalked off with the man holding the fuel cell.

She looked at Ren.

He knelt there in the dirt, yet seemed so calm.

She was about to have a panic attack. They were going to be executed.

Then he winked at her.

What the hell?

CHAPTER SIXTEEN

Ren steadied himself.

It was hard to stay focused when that asshole had Halle. When she was in danger.

But this was what he was good at. He had the skills to save his woman.

The two men with the fuel cell walked away, their footsteps fading. The two men left to execute them, were talking.

Halle looked like she was about to lose it. He winked at her. He saw her startled look, but she stayed still.

One masked man stepped in front of Ren, a gun in his hand.

Ren released a slow breath. His plan depended on the element of surprise.

He remembered how he'd operated in Ghost Ops. *Never quit. Never stop. You're never out of the fight.*

Now, apart from his training and skills, he also had the added motivation of saving Halle.

He leaped up, and his hard blow chopped into the

attacker's arm. The gun went flying. He turned and punched Halle's captor in the face with one hand, and knocked the knife away from her skin with the other.

The man staggered backward, and Ren yanked Halle away from the man.

"Duck," he ordered.

She obeyed without hesitation.

Ren was already whirling to attack the first man.

The asshole came in fast, with quick blows. Ren snapped his hands up, blocking the hits. The guy was swift and agile, but Ren was taller. He used that to his advantage. He leaned over and rammed his fingers into the man's eyes.

He made a pained sound, and they whirled. Ren shoved the man into the second attacker who was advancing again.

The pair went down in the dirt in a tangle.

Ren strode forward, scooped up a dropped handgun, and aimed.

Bang. Bang.

Neither man moved.

If their friends had heard the shots, they'd think it was the men executing Halle and Ren.

He turned.

Halle swallowed. "You're like Liam Neeson in *Taken*, just younger and hotter."

The shock of humor made him grin at her. "How can you make me laugh right now?"

She ran to him, and he wrapped his arms around her. Then he ran a finger over her face, rubbing away the blood from the cut.

"He cut you."

"Barely." She pressed a gentle hand to his cheek. "I'm just really glad we're still alive."

He leaned into that touch. That softness. It was what he'd been missing. Denying himself.

"Thank you for killing to save me." Then her face turned stricken. "Ren, the fuel cell. They have the fuel cell."

"Then we'd better get it back. Grab the backpack and whatever gear you can salvage."

While Halle did that, he checked the weapon and cursed. It was out of ammo. Quickly, he checked the bodies of the two men. No more ammo. *Dammit.* He did find a thin wire in one man's pocket. A garrote wire. He slipped it into his own pocket.

"Come on, stay right behind me." He tossed the weapon into the trees.

They crept quietly in the direction the other men had gone. The trees petered out, and he spotted a dark-colored SUV parked ahead. The two men were there. The boss guy was leaning against the hood, talking on a cellphone. No doubt checking in with the rest of his team.

"Halle, get down," Ren murmured quietly.

She huddled behind a large, spiky bush. He saw the other man open the back of the SUV, putting the fuel cell in a silver case.

"Wait here."

She nodded.

Then Ren moved through the trees. Silent. Stealthy. He dragged in a deep breath. He felt like he was back in Ghost Ops. Following Vander, with Boone and Shep beside him. Sawyer and the others bringing up the rear.

He paused. The boss was still talking on the phone. Ren advanced on the man at the rear of the vehicle, pulling the garrote wire out of his pocket. He crept in, moving fast.

He whipped the wire over the man's head and yanked it hard against his throat.

Ren pulled hard enough that the guy made no sound. He clutched the wire for a few seconds, tearing at it as he kicked his feet. Ren gritted his teeth and held on until the man sagged.

With a bend of his knees, Ren put his shoulder into the man's gut and lifted him onto his shoulder. He could still hear the other man talking.

He reached into the back of the SUV and grabbed the fuel cell, then he quickly darted back into the trees.

He found some dense bushes and dumped the body in them. Then he hurried back to Halle.

"The guy doesn't even know what happened yet," Halle whispered, nodding toward the boss guy. "You're amazing."

Ren felt a flush of warmth in his chest. He took the backpack from her and set the fuel cell back inside. "How about we get out of here?"

"I think that sounds like an excellent idea."

HALLE RAN BEHIND REN. They were heading down the hill and the trees were thinning out. The grass was now knee-deep, slowing them down.

The way he'd taken out those men…

She'd seen the warrior inside him. She knew he'd do anything to keep her safe.

They went a bit farther when she spotted the road. Elation filled her.

Ren helped her over a wire fence. Hills rose up off in the distance, covered in a smattering of trees and vegetation. In the other direction, the road headed toward the ocean.

"That way." Ren pointed toward the water.

"There's still more of them, right?"

"Yes." He squeezed her hand. "But I'm not letting them touch you."

They hadn't been walking long when she had the rumble of an engine. Ren froze and grabbed her arm.

Halle's pulse was pounding. "Is it them?"

His gaze narrowed as he stared back up the road. "I don't think so."

A moment later the vehicle came into view. It was a red, soft-top Jeep. There were surfboards poking out the back and she could hear music blaring.

Ren raised an arm and waved. The Jeep pulled over, spraying gravel nearby.

There were two young men in the front who had "surfer" stamped all over them.

The one driving had shaggy black hair and was wearing a faded Corona T-shirt. The passenger had long, sun-bleached hair pulled back into a messy man bun. His

Hawaiian shirt seared her eyeballs—it was a tropical mix of red, green, yellow, and hot pink.

"You guys okay?" the driver asked with a distinct Australian accent.

"We need a ride to the closest town," Ren said.

"Sure. Get in."

Ren helped Halle climb into the back seat of the Jeep.

A moment later, their new friends took off down the road. The passenger turned down the music and looked back at them. "I'm Matt. This is Jordy." Unlike his friend, Matt was an American.

"You're surfers?" Halle asked.

"Sure are," Matt said. "We're always chasing a good wave. Not much on this side of Molokai. We just thought we'd go for a drive today."

"Do some exploring," Jordy added.

"There are decent waves on the other side of Molokai." Matt cocked his head. "You guys on vacation?"

"Not exactly," Halle said.

Ren leaned forward. "Do either of you have a cellphone? Could I borrow it?"

Matt shrugged. "Sure. As long as you don't call overseas or anything." He fished around in the pocket of his board shorts, then handed it over.

With a nod, Ren took the phone and dialed a number. "Sawyer—" he paused "—yeah, we're alive. We have the fuel cell." Another pause. "Somewhere on the eastern side of Molokai." He paused. "Yes. There's a team on the ground tracking us. Chinese." Ren glanced around. "We hitched a ride and we're on..."

"Hawaii State Route 450," Jordy called back. "The Kamehameha V Highway. Not far from Fagan's Beach."

Ren relayed the information to his friend.

Matt looked at Halle. "You guys in trouble?"

She nodded. "There's a team of people, probably Chinese agents, after us. They're not very friendly."

Matt's eyes widened. "Wow."

"No shit?" Jordy said.

She tilted her head. "You're both very chill about it."

"That's our motto," Matt said. "Always be chill. Still, Chinese secret agents chasing you... Crazy."

Halle heard the sound of engines.

She looked back, and her heart leaped into her throat. She saw three black SUVs in the distance.

They were still a fair way off, but were gaining on them.

"Sawyer, I have to go." Ren handed the phone back to Matt. "Thanks."

"Dudes, I think we have company," Jordy said.

A muscle ticked in Ren's jaw. "Let us out ahead."

"You sure? This baby—" Jordy patted the dash "—has some speed. We can try and outrun them."

"I don't want to put you in danger. These men won't hesitate to kill."

Matt swallowed. "That's not cool."

At the next corner, Jordy pulled over.

Halle saw three large houses ahead, perched on the hillside overlooking the water. Ren leaped out, then helped her.

"Thanks for the ride," she said.

"Go," Ren told the young men. "They'll see that

you've let us out. Drive and don't stop. Hide somewhere on the other side of the island."

The men nodded.

"Good luck," Matt said.

Halle swallowed. Something told her that she and Ren would need it.

CHAPTER SEVENTEEN

Ren and Halle jogged toward the three houses. He scanned around and didn't see any cars.

"They're probably holiday homes," he said.

Halle glanced back over her shoulder. "They'll be here soon. What should we do? Should we hide?"

"No." He wanted to be somewhere where he had some advantage. "I think we'll make a stand."

"What did your friend Sawyer say?"

"Vander had already called him. He's been on standby waiting to hear from me."

"He'll come to help us?"

"Yes. But I'm not sure how long it'll take him to get here. I didn't have long enough to hear his plan." Ren's best guess was that it was at least a thirty-minute flight between Maui and Molokai.

Ren's gaze locked onto the large house farthest away from the road.

"Come on." He jogged toward the house. It had

brown siding and white-framed windows. There was a small front porch framed by some garden beds.

Ignoring the front door, they circled around the side of the house.

"Oh, wow." Halle's steps slowed and she stopped to take in the view. The house sat above a perfect curve of beach. There were palm trees, and waves lapping at the pristine sand. It was a small slice of paradise.

Ren spotted a side door and peered through the glass. It led into a laundry room. He lifted his boot and kicked the door in.

He ushered Halle inside. They hurried down a hallway, footsteps echoing on the wooden floor. They stepped into the open plan living and kitchen area. It was open and airy, with a wide deck overlooking the ocean. The house was decorated like it was a holiday rental—generic furniture, stylish decor.

"Ren, how can you fight them? You don't have a gun." She threw out an arm. "They'll have an arsenal and you'll be outnumbered."

He saw the panic in her eyes and cupped her cheeks. "Baby, this is what I was trained to do. I don't need a gun. There are plenty of weapons here that I can use."

Ren strode to the kitchen sink. He yanked open a cupboard beneath it, and pulled out some bottles of cleaning chemicals. There was a bottle of bleach, a can of fly spray, some glass cleaner. He set them on the countertop.

Halle frowned at him.

Next, he opened the drawers, and found several knives. Those went onto the countertop as well.

Spinning, he strode into the dining room. There was a heavy glass vase in the center of the table, and he tested its weight. He nodded.

Then he headed down the hall. Halle followed behind him.

He stepped into the bathroom. He took a second to note the clean, white tiles, open shower stall to the left, and large tub to the right. Under the vanity, he found a can of hairspray, a candle, and a lighter. He set them beside the sink. Then he leaned over the bathtub, set the plug in place, and flicked the tap on.

"What are you doing?" she asked.

"Preparing for battle."

When there were several inches of water in the tub, he turned the tap off.

Next, he strode into the closest bedroom while Halle hovered in the doorway. It was clearly the main bedroom, with a large king bed that was currently stripped back to the mattress. There were blinds on the window, and he opened them, lengthening the cords dangling from them. They'd do.

"Ren?" She swiveled. "I can hear cars pulling up."

He grabbed her arm, and they hurried back into the living room. Outside, tires crunched on gravel, and he heard voices.

Ren peered out the front window.

He saw the SUVs, and the men spilling out of them.

Show time.

Turning, he hurried Halle back into the dining area. He glanced around and his gaze fell on the large flat-screen TV resting on a large cabinet. It was made of a lightweight wood with wicker insets in the doors.

Perfect. She'd fit and she'd be able to breathe.

He opened the cabinet on the left. He pulled out several things inside—place mats, a large bowl, cloth napkins—and stuffed them into the right-hand side.

"You need to hide, Halle." He gestured to the cabinet. "Whatever you hear or see, *don't* come out until I come to get you."

"Ren." She pressed her hands to his chest.

He kissed her—hard and quick.

"It's going to be fine." He tipped her chin up. "It's my honor to fight for you. To protect you. I think it was what I was born to do."

She lifted her hand to his cheek. "You do what you have to do, but you stay safe. You come back to me."

He nodded, then slipped off the backpack and pressed it into her arms.

She climbed into the cabinet. It was a tight fit and she had to curl her knees up to her chest.

He crouched in front of her. "Stay still and quiet."

She nodded.

Then he closed the door behind her and turned. He heard voices at the front door.

He pulled in a deep breath, and let battle mode settle over him.

Defeat the enemy. Protect his country. Defend his woman.

Let's do this.

He slipped down the hall and into the bedroom. He slid the mirrored closet door open and stepped inside. He closed the door most of the way, just leaving it open a crack.

It wasn't long before he heard footsteps.

That's it. Just a little farther.

The masked man entered the room quietly. He was holding a handgun.

He searched the room, and checked under the bed. Then he came toward the closet.

Just another step.

There.

Ren shoved the door open, and grabbed the blind cord. The man was whirling toward him, but he was too slow.

Ren whipped the cord around to the man's throat. He used all his strength to pull it tight.

The man fought desperately, the blinds slapping against the wall. His gun dropped from nerveless fingers, and he struggled to get free.

Ren pulled harder.

Finally, the man slumped over. Ren lowered the attacker's dead weight to the ground, then snatched up the man's gun. It was a QSZ-92. The pistol used by the Chinese military.

He slipped it into the waistband of his shorts. It was a last resort. If he fired it, it would attract the others searching the other houses.

He moved into the hall, and saw another man at the end in the kitchen.

Ren moved quietly, but the man lifted his head and spotted him. He shouted.

Fuck.

Ren ducked into the bathroom. He snatched up the hairspray and lighter.

The attacker burst into the room.

Ren sprayed and ignited the chemical.

The flames hit the man in the face and his mask caught fire.

The man screamed and clawed at his head.

Ren dropped the can, then pressed a hand to the back of the man's neck. He shoved, ramming the attacker's face into the marble vanity.

Crack. The man went limp and dropped to the floor. The flames had died out and he didn't move.

Two down.

ALL SHE COULD HEAR WAS the loud thud of her heart.

Halle could just see through the wicker. At least she wasn't locked in the dark.

She heard footsteps and her chest hitched.

Two men moved into the living room.

God. Please let Ren be all right. There was a lump in her throat the size of a boulder.

One man moved out of sight. Then she heard a noise and froze.

The second man was *right* in front of the TV cabinet.

Oh. Hell.

She didn't move. She didn't dare breathe. She clenched her fingers together.

He walked past her—slowly and silently.

If he found her, she'd be dead.

She closed her eyes.

It will be fine. Ren is with you.

They were going to get through this.

She wanted a life with him. She wanted shared dinners and cotton candy, to watch corny black and white TV shows in bed together, and she wanted more toe-curling, delicious sex.

She wanted Ren.

The intruder continued on. He walked past the dining table, his gloved hand trailing across the wooden surface. He moved into the kitchen.

Suddenly, a dark shape exploded out of the hallway and rammed into the man.

Ren.

She sucked in a breath, pressing her eye closer to the wicker to get a better view.

Ren and the man grappled, and they rammed into the island. She heard their grunts and harsh expulsions of breath.

They whirled again, trading punches. Then Ren stepped back and grabbed the bottle of bleach off the countertop. He snapped the lid off, and threw the chemical at the man.

The attacker screamed.

Ren lunged and grabbed two knives off the island. He launched at the man.

Halle looked away.

When the sounds stopped, she saw Ren standing in the center of the kitchen, his chest heaving.

All of a sudden, another man ran into the room.

Ren whirled and threw a knife, but the man dodged. He was so fast.

The man leaped onto the table, ran three steps, and jumped.

Ren rolled under him, spun, and attacked him with the knife. His arm slashed out.

But the attacker had clearly been trained in some sort of martial arts. He came at Ren with a flurry of kicks and chops.

The attacker's boot connected with Ren's wrist, the knife went flying into the air.

Ren raised his arms, blocking several hits. He punched the man in the gut.

They collided, and crashed into a chair at the table, knocking it over. She heard grunting and straining.

Suddenly, the attacker shoved free, then slammed Ren against the table on his back. His hands clamped on Ren's neck, and he squeezed.

No.

Ren bucked, trying to get free, but the man was strong.

Come on, Ren.

She saw Ren reaching across the table, trying to grab the glass vase. His fingers slapped against the wood.

She had to help him.

Gathering up her courage, she pushed the backpack down to the bottom of the cabinet. Then she threw the door open and surged out.

Halle ran two steps. The man was turning toward her when she grabbed the vase.

She lifted it high, then smashed it into his head.

He groaned, staggering backward. Ren surged up. He landed several rapid punches that sent the man to his knees.

She pressed a hand to her chest, over her thundering heart, and watched Ren ram his knee into the man's face.

The masked attacker slumped to the ground.

Ren's gaze sliced her way. "You were supposed to stay in the cabinet."

"I wasn't going to sit there and let him strangle you to death."

"The fuel cell?"

"It's still in the cabinet." She hurried over, reached in, and grabbed the backpack.

Voices outside had both of their heads whipping up.

Ren cursed. "We have more company incoming. Come on."

He pulled her into the hallway. She saw the bloody body in the kitchen and quickly looked away. There was another body on the bathroom floor. *God.*

When she saw movement out of the corner of her eye, she jerked her head up.

A masked man charged into the hallway. He'd come through the laundry room door they'd used earlier. He raised his gun and aimed at them.

Oh, no.

Ren shouldered into Halle, driving her into the bathroom.

CHAPTER EIGHTEEN

Ren caught his balance as Halle tripped over the dead body of the man on the floor. She tumbled into the open shower stall.

He turned, stepped to the side, and lifted his hands.

The attacker came through the door and fired his weapon. Blocking out the deafening sound of the gunshot, Ren slammed the door into him.

The gun dropped to the tiles.

Ren grabbed the front of the man's shirt and yanked him in. He swiveled, and the man tried to hit Ren, but Ren shoved him hard. Then, using all his strength, he jerked the man around and shoved him forward.

The attacker tried hard to get free. Ren used all his weight to force the man to his knees.

Gritting his teeth, Ren shoved the man's head into the water in the bathtub.

There was an explosion of bubbles as the man fought. He tried to shove back, but Ren held on. The bastard was strong.

The man's next, desperate shove nearly knocked Ren off him. Dammit, he wasn't sure he could hold him.

Then a second set of hands joined Ren's.

He turned his head. "Halle—"

She added her weight and strength to his. "Together."

They held the man down until the bubbles stopped and his body went slack.

Chest heaving, Ren hauled her up and away from the dead man. He was so damn sorry she'd had to be a part of this. Sorry that any of this had happened to her.

All he could focus on now was getting her to safety.

"Let's go." He grabbed the man's dropped assault rifle. They hurried out to the kitchen, and into the living room.

"Stay against the wall," he warned.

She pressed her back to the wall. Her face was pale, but she was holding it together.

Ren peeked outside through the front window.

He saw several more attackers coming out of the other houses. They were pointing at the house Ren and Halle were in.

All of them were carrying automatic weapons.

"We need to go," he said urgently. "Out the back. *Now.*"

He pushed her ahead of him.

Then gunfire ripped into the front of the house.

Halle screamed. Windows shattered and wood splintered.

Ren tackled her to the floor, covering her body with his. Glass sprinkled over them.

"Crawl to the sliding door," he said in her ear.

She nodded, pushed up on her hands and knees, and crawled fast. He moved right behind her.

When they reached the sliding doors, he yanked it open. "Up."

Together, they ran out onto the deck.

"We need to get down to the beach." There was a winding path down to the sea.

Halle grabbed the straps of the backpack, and jogged down the steps of the deck.

Ren checked behind them. Their attackers were still shooting at the front of the house. He needed a plan. They could get to the beach, but then what? His jaw tightened.

Whatever happened, Halle was getting out of here alive.

They hustled down the winding path to the beach. They were almost there when he heard shouts behind them.

He saw their attackers spilling out onto the deck.

"Halle! Run faster."

She picked up speed and he sprinted after her. Gunshots peppered the ground around them, hitting the sandy ground.

He whirled and fired up at the deck. He saw the attackers dive for cover.

"Keep running."

Halle pumped her arms and legs. More shots were fired from the house, and he cursed.

Then, Ren saw her jerk and go down.

His world stopped.

"Halle!" he roared.

He raced toward her. Pain lanced the top of his shoulder and he stumbled.

Dammit, he'd been hit. He locked the pain down. All his focus was on Halle.

He reached her, just as she rolled over. There was blood on her arm.

"I'm okay," she said breathlessly. "I think."

He hauled her up. It looked like she'd been nicked.

The air rushed out of him, and the searing relief made him lightheaded. He kept his body between hers and the house.

"Get to the beach. I'll buy us some time."

Her face twisted. "Ren—"

"I'll be right behind you, baby. I promise."

HALLE RAN AS FAST as she could.

Her lungs were burning, her arm was stinging, and blood was soaking her sleeve.

She heard more gunfire behind her and knew Ren was firing on their pursuers.

She grimaced. *God.*

Her feet hit the sand. The waves were lapping nearby. It was a picturesque paradise, except for the gunfire and the foreign agents after them.

Not to mention the fuel cell that felt heavy on her back.

"Come to Hawaii," she muttered. "For rest and relaxation."

Chest heaving, she hurried along the beach. She wondered where the hell they would go.

"Halle!"

A familiar male voice made her spin in shock.

"God, Halle, are you okay?"

She stared wide-eyed as she watched Professor Davis running out of the palm trees.

"Professor?" She couldn't compute his presence. "How did you get here? How...?" Realization hit, hollowing her out. "It was you."

The professor stopped, and swiped an arm across his face.

"*You* sold us out," she said. "You're working with the Chinese."

"Halle." His face crumpled.

"It's your own project! How could you?"

Ren sprinted down the beach. "Get back, Halle." He aimed his rifle at the professor.

"Do you have the fuel cell?" Professor Davis asked. "Please. Give it to me."

"Are the rest of our team all right?" Halle asked. "Or are they dead?"

"They're fine." Sweat poured down his face. "Give me the fuel cell."

"How did they get to you?" Ren asked. "Money?"

Davis pinched the bridge of his nose. "They offered me a lot of money." He swallowed. "But that's not why I'm doing this. They have incriminating photos of me." He looked at the sand, and swallowed. "Of me and an undergraduate student."

Halle made a noise. "You sold us out because you slept with a student?"

"A male student." Professor Davis threw up his hands. "I'm married. I have a family and a reputation—"

"That you made the choice to ruin," Halle said. "You man up and face what you did. You don't turn into a traitor and help a foreign country."

"Give me the fuel cell," he said desperately.

"And you tried to frame me," Halle continued, the betrayal cutting deep. "You wanted my access code so no one would suspect you."

"I need the fuel cell." He lunged for her.

Bang.

Professor Davis cried out and clutched his leg. He went down on the sand, moaning. Ren stared at him impassively, and lowered his gun.

Her heart hit her ribs. Ren took her hand and pulled her along the beach.

"Ren, where are we going to go?" That's when she saw the blood on the top of his left shoulder. "Oh my, God, you were hit." Her throat closed. "*God.*"

"The bullet cut a groove over my shoulder, it's fine. How's your arm?"

"I don't even feel it." She shook her head. She felt sand slide into her shoes. "Ren, I can't believe it was Professor Davis. He was behind all of this."

Ren met her gaze. "People make terrible decisions and do terrible things all the time, Halle."

Her heart squeezed. She knew he was thinking of Nasrin, and the people who'd hurt her.

Then he glanced back behind them.

She looked too. More men were running down the path toward the beach. Her belly clutched. "They're coming."

"I know." He dragged in a deep breath. "You need to swim out to sea. I know you're a strong swimmer. Take the fuel cell, and swim as far as you can. Get away from here."

"*No.*" She shook her head wildly. "I'm *not* leaving you."

"I need to keep them occupied to give you a chance. Halle—" he cupped her cheeks "—I love you."

Her eyes went wide. God, it felt so good to hear him say those words. "You love me?"

"I love you, Halle Bradshaw. The most important thing to me is that you're safe."

She pressed her hands over his. "I love you too, Ren. So much. And what's important to me, is that we're together."

At the end of the beach, their attackers reached the sand.

They were out of time.

"Run!" Ren shoved her.

They sprinted along the beach and helplessness choked her.

They had nowhere to go. They'd run out of beach soon.

She heard more gunfire.

Life could be so cruel. She'd lost her mom. And now, just as she'd gotten Ren, just when he'd told her that he loved her, they were going to die.

It wasn't fair.

Ren stopped, and fired back down the beach.

But there were too many of them. They kept coming.

Ren turned and wrapped his arms around her. She pressed her face to his chest.

"I'm sorry, Halle." His palm cupped the back of her head.

"Ren—"'

They were together. A sense of calm washed over her. She was with the man she loved.

Suddenly, there was a loud roar.

For a second, Halle thought their attackers had unleashed some new weapon.

Then, a helicopter thundered overhead.

Halle gasped. She looked up and saw *Sheriff* emblazoned in gold on the side of the black-and-white helicopter.

A second helicopter followed. It was larger, and pale-gray colored. This one had Navy on the tail.

"Oh, God." A crazy mix of emotions filled her.

Ren pulled her closer and grinned. "Looks like help arrived just in time."

CHAPTER NINETEEN

Ren stared up at the helicopter and saw his buddy Sawyer in the open side door. The former Ghost Ops soldier had a rifle in his hand. He lifted, aimed, and fired at the attackers racing onto the beach.

Swiveling, Ren saw several of the masked men go down. Sawyer had always been a good shot. It was that patience of his.

In the distance, Ren heard the sound of sirens.

More help arriving.

Relief punched through him. *They'd made it.*

Halle was safe.

Halle laughed and dropped to her knees. "We're going to be all right."

"I promised you we would be." He dropped down in front of her.

The Navy helicopter flew over the houses, and he heard more gunfire. Meanwhile, the Sheriff's helicopter came into land on the sand nearby.

As the wind whipped at their hair, Halle cupped his

cheeks. Her face lit up. Her smile was so beautiful and his chest tightened. Damn, he loved her.

With a happy sound, she kissed him.

He hauled her closer and kissed her back. He kept kissing her. He never wanted to stop.

"I swing in to save the day, and you still get the girl," a deep voice said.

Ren looked up and saw Sawyer standing over them in his sheriff's uniform.

Dark green pants covered long legs, and his khaki shirt stretched over a wide chest. His service weapon was holstered at his hip. Sawyer had light brown hair he kept cut short, although it was longer than the last time Ren had seen him, and the tips were turning gold. Clearly, Hawaii agreed with him.

He had a strong jaw, and Ren had always teased him about having a Superman jaw, complete with a dent in the center of his chin. He often got mistaken for the actor who played Jack Reacher in the TV show. Ren found it hilarious, and Sawyer found it annoying.

Right now, Sawyer was smiling, his green eyes alight with amusement.

Ren pulled Halle up. "Sawyer. About time you got here." With one arm, he hugged his friend, and Sawyer slapped his back.

"Just glad you aren't riddled with bullets."

"Me too." Ren tucked Halle under his arm. "Deputy Sheriff Sawyer Lane, meet Halle Bradshaw. Halle, this is my good friend, Sawyer."

Halle reached out and hugged Sawyer. "We are *very* glad to see you."

Sawyer gently patted her back. "Glad you're okay, Halle."

"How did you get here so fast?" Ren asked.

"I didn't have time to tell you when you called that I was already on the island," Sawyer answered. "After we learned that the *Atalanta* had been attacked, I decided to try and track you down."

"How did you know about the *Atalanta*?" Ren asked.

"Your man, Damien, managed to get a message out."

Ren shook his head. "That man is getting a raise."

"After his call, I mobilized. A Coast Guard MSST team secured your ship and took the attackers into custody."

Ren knew that the Coast Guard's Maritime Safety and Security Team were experts at infiltrating ships.

Sawyer glanced at Halle. "Your team are all okay, by the way." Then his face turned serious as he looked at Ren. "You lost a few of your crew."

Ren thought of Jack. "I saw one was dead when we got away. He was a good man."

"We learned that you and Halle had left with the drone and fuel cell. And Mark Davis was missing. We figured you'd aim for the closest island, so I scrambled what resources I could." A smile tugged at Sawyer's lips. "I wasn't having much luck at first, but Vander pulled a few strings. Suddenly, the sheriff offered me a helo, and the Navy were all too happy to help as well. They were very motivated to get their fuel cell back. We came to Molokai to find you."

"God, it's over," Halle said. "We're safe. We're alive."

Ren cupped the back of her neck. "We are, baby."

With a whoop, she leaped on him. His hands cupped her ass as she wrapped her legs around his hips and kissed him.

Damn. His cock twitched. He really wished they didn't have an audience.

Then he sensed something and broke the kiss.

He looked up and saw a group heading down the beach toward them.

Instantly, from the way three of the men moved, he knew they were Navy SEALs. No doubt from Pearl Harbor.

Then his gaze fell on the dark-haired man striding at the front of the group. He wore a ballistic vest and was carrying an assault rifle.

Vander Norcross.

The man beside Vander jerked to a stop, staring at Ren and Halle.

Ren sucked in a breath.

Tom.

As the rest of the group continued down the path, Tom stood frozen, his face impassive.

Oh, hell.

Halle looked over and blinked. "Dad."

Ren set her down. He'd known this moment would come. He took her hand.

She was his, and he wanted everyone to know, and that included Tom.

Ren best's friend and mentor stared at them for another second, then swiveled, and stalked back up the hill toward the houses.

"*Oh.*" Halle looked distraught.

"It's going to be okay," Ren murmured. "I love you."

That got him a smile.

"Ren," a deep voice said.

Ren looked up and into the dark eyes of his former commander. A man he trusted to the bone. "Vander."

Vander pulled him in for a quick hug. "Damn glad you're all right, Ren."

He realized Vander must have left for Hawaii not long after he'd spoken with him on the *Atalanta*. "You didn't have to come."

Vander's lips quirked. "Yeah. I did. I had an inkling you'd need some help."

"Thank fuck for your spooky instincts. Things were getting dire."

"You left a trail of bodies up there." Vander jerked a thumb at the house.

"I wasn't letting any of them get to Halle."

Vander smiled. "It's a pleasure to see you, Halle."

She held out a hand. "Thanks for your help. And thanks for having Ren's back."

Vander nodded and looked at Ren. "You finally got your head out of your ass."

Ren laughed. "I did." He pulled her against his chest and wrapped an arm around her neck. "I couldn't fight her any longer."

"And the fuel cell?" Vander asked.

"*Oh.*" Halle slipped the backpack off her shoulders and pulled it open.

Ren reached in and pulled the fuel cell out.

"Well done, both of you." Vander took it, then

handed it to one of the Navy SEALs. "You did good work."

At the end of the beach, Ren saw the other two SEALs had several Chinese men in handcuffs, as well as Professor Davis. And several local law enforcement officers were heading down the beach path.

"You two look like you need a hot shower and a few days of sleep," Sawyer said.

Halle groaned. "I have to say my first time on a Hawaiian island didn't quite go how I expected. A hot shower sounds like heaven.

"I think that can be arranged," Sawyer said with a smile. "I promise, we can show you the better side of Hawaii."

REN WAS silent as they walked up the path from the beach.

And not in a good way.

Halle had a sick feeling building inside her.

"Ren..." She stopped. "I know we need to talk to my father."

"Yes."

God, clearly her father had been shocked and surprised to see her and Ren together. What if he demanded Ren leave her? What if her stubborn man agreed out of misguided guilt?

"Hey." Ren gripped her chin. "I love you. You're the best thing that ever walked into my life. I love your dad, too. I owe him so much."

She bit her lip, feeling like she was waiting for an axe to drop.

"But I'm *not* giving you up." He lowered his head and kissed her. "You're mine, and I'll face down endless foreign agents, unhappy fathers, or whatever comes my way. I'd go to war for you."

She went up on her toes and nibbled his lips. "Let's hope it doesn't come to that."

Hand in hand, they circled the house. It was looking very worse for wear. There were broken windows and bullet holes everywhere. She winced, thinking of the poor owners.

There were several police cars out front, and she saw several hard-eyed prisoners on the ground, along with quite a few sheet-covered bodies. The Navy helicopter sat nearby.

It was a Sikorsky Seahawk. Her father had made her memorize Navy ships and aircraft as a game when she'd been little.

Then her gaze fell on the tall form of her father. He stood nearby, with his back to them, facing the ocean, and his hands on his hips. The breeze teased his brown hair that was the same color as hers, except where the gray had started to creep in.

Halle took hold of Ren's hand, set her shoulders back, then strode toward her father.

"Dad?"

His shoulders tensed, then he turned. His jaw was tight.

"Are you all right, Halle?" His gaze fell on their joined hands and his lips flattened.

"Just a few scrapes and bruises," she said.

"She got nicked by a bullet," Ren added.

"What?" Her dad grabbed her shoulders.

"I'm fine, Dad."

He sucked in a harsh breath. "Thank God." He pressed his forehead to hers. "I've been so worried. As soon as I heard there was a problem, I flew out here."

Love filled her. This man had always been there for her. He'd missed a lot during her younger years, but he was still the one who'd taught her to ride a bike, taught her self-defense, made her hot dogs when her first boyfriend had broken up with her. After her mom had died, he'd never wavered in supporting her.

Then he looked up and his gaze locked on Ren.

"You asshole," her dad bit out. "I trusted you. I asked you to look after her, and you..."

Ren said nothing.

Halle huffed out a breath. "Dad—"

"*No.*" Her father shook his head. "He's my best friend. The man I trusted most in the entire world. He broke the unwritten code. I was worried sick about the both of you, but I knew Ren would have your back. And then I see you two kissing."

"*Dad,*" she tried again.

"He's older and more experienced than you. He took advantage of you. He—"

"Fell in love with me," she said.

Her father startled at the vehemence in her voice

"And I'm in love with him," she said softly. "I have been for a long while, but he's been fighting it."

Something shifted in his father's eyes, and he glanced at Ren. "That's why you haven't come around so much."

"Dad, I'm standing here alive and unharmed because of him. Because he risked everything to keep me safe." She reached back and took Ren's hand. Their fingers tangled. "I love him. And you love him. Who better for me to be with, Dad? Than the man you trust, love, and respect."

Her father raked a hand through his hair. "No one's good enough for my little girl."

She smiled. "I'm not so little anymore."

Ren took a step forward. "I'll do everything to make her happy, Tom. And keep her safe. To give her everything she wants and deserves."

"*Fuck.*" Her dad muttered. Emotions crossed his face. "Come here."

He pulled both Halle and Ren in for a hug.

She threw her arms around both the men she loved.

"I love you, Halle," her father said. "You've always been the light of my life." He looked at Ren. "It has been an honor to watch you grow into the man you are today. Take care of my girl."

Ren gave him a solemn nod. She could tell he was holding back his own emotions. She wrapped her arms around him and pressed her face to his chest.

Then her father lowered his voice. "If you ever make her unhappy, I'll gut you. Quickly, quietly, and your body will never be found."

"*Dad.*" She slapped his stomach. "That is a bad joke."

"It's not a joke," Ren said.

She blinked.

Then both men smiled and hugged again, slapping each other's backs.

Love welled in Halle, for both of them. Her warriors. Her father, and the man who'd captured her heart.

She saw Sawyer and Vander standing nearby. If she wasn't already in love with Ren, she'd definitely spend some time checking them out.

"When can we get out of here?" she asked.

"As soon as you're ready, baby." Ren ran a hand over her hair.

"How about you come back to Maui with me?" Sawyer suggested. "We'll get you guys checked out, then I'll show you some real Hawaiian hospitality."

"As long as it involves no hikes through jungles, no long ocean swims, and no bad guys, I'm in," she said.

Her father smiled at her, and Ren laughed and pressed a kiss to the top of her head.

CHAPTER TWENTY

Ren woke to the sound of gentle waves lapping on the shore, and bright Hawaiian sunlight seeping around the curtains.

And the feel of warm hands tugging at his boxer shorts.

He looked down and saw Halle press a kiss to his stomach. His muscles clenched. Her loose, silky brown hair was everywhere. He slid a hand into it and tugged it to the side so he could see her pretty face. She smiled up at him.

Damn, she made him feel so damn much.

Then she circled his cock, closed her mouth over the top, and sucked him into her mouth.

He groaned. "My girl loves sucking my cock." His words made her suck harder. He let her play, every muscle clenched to stop from coming in her sweet mouth.

When he couldn't handle it anymore, he pulled her off and dragged her up his body.

"Good morning." He kissed her plump lips.

"I wasn't quite finished." She sank her teeth into his bottom lip.

They were on Maui. Sawyer's cousin lived on the island and had married a Hawaiian woman. It seemed her family had welcomed Sawyer like one of their own. Halle and Ren were staying in a holiday villa owned by... someone in the extended family. Ren couldn't remember everyone's names.

The villa was small, but pretty, and perched right on the beach.

Halle's lips moved along his jaw. Then she shifted and kissed the bandage on his shoulder. After their rescue on Molokai, they'd both been checked out by paramedics. Halle had a matching bandage on her arm.

She was safe.

That thought kept echoing in his head.

He planned to keep it that way. He was not going to let her out of his sight.

They'd also been debriefed, and the Chinese agents, along with Mark Davis had been whisked away to who knew where to be interrogated.

Halle looked up at him. "Love you."

He slid a hand into her hair. "I love you too. You'll never know how much."

"*Ren...*"

"Everything I saw and did. Every fight, every loss, every sacrifice, this makes it worthwhile. You make it worthwhile."

Tears welled in her eyes.

He touched her cheeks. "These better be happy tears."

She sniffed. "They are."

He stroked the silky strands of her hair. "So sweet and smart and beautiful. Loves cotton candy, and old corny TV shows. Loves dolphins—"

"And sharks," she added with a smile.

Love overflowed inside him. "And sharks."

She straddled him, her pretty breasts in his face. She shimmied against him.

Ren groaned. "We can't. We're meeting Tom for a late breakfast, remember?"

After Molokai, Vander had flown back to the mainland. Tom had come with them to Maui. Ren suspected the man needed some more time to reassure himself that Halle was all right.

Halle's lips attacked Ren's earlobe, her slick pussy rubbing against his cock.

"We have time," she murmured.

He groaned again. "But he'll take one look at you and know I fucked you." He clamped his hands on his waist, and got distracted by her soft skin.

She rubbed again, and he could feel how wet she was.

"He's going to have to get used to that," she murmured.

With a growl, Ren rolled her under him. She was too tempting, and all his. He closed his mouth over hers and nudged her thighs apart.

"Hold on, baby. This isn't going to be slow or gentle."

Her smile was slow and sexy. "Good."

CRADLING HIS BEER, Ren watched the sunset. They were at a small, local restaurant which was still currently empty, but there were great smells coming from the kitchen.

"So, the great Lorenzo Santoro has fallen."

Ren glanced at Sawyer beside him. His friend was wearing jeans and a T-shirt, a beer bottle dangling from his fingers.

"Yeah, he has," Ren said.

"You look happy about it. Once, I remember you telling me there were too many beautiful fish in the sea, and you'd never let yourself get hooked."

"I was an idiot," Ren said.

Sawyer cocked his head. "No, you don't just look happy about it, you look...right."

"I never expected to fall in love. Or wanted it."

"You always were stubborn." Sawyer sipped his beer.

Ren spotted Halle and Tom. They were walking in the gardens. Halle wore a flowing dress, with a hibiscus flower tucked behind her ear.

He'd never be good enough for her, but she was his. No matter what.

Someone called out Halle's name and Ren looked over. Sammy, Fitz, and Ryan were walking over. Sammy was holding two cocktails with leaves, flowers, and umbrellas sticking out the top.

The three scientists had joined them that morning, eager to be reunited with Halle.

"God, she's amazing, Sawyer. It's not just the big stuff. It's the small stuff too. She just has to smile at me, and the world feels lighter."

"First Vander got married. Then Boone and Shep fell in love with their women, now you." Sawyer shook his head. "I hope it's not catching."

"Sawyer—" Ren grabbed his friend's arm. "Don't cut yourself off from living."

Sawyer chuckled. "Ren, I've got lots of friends here. I'm a part of the community, whether I want to be or not."

Ren shook his head. "I know how easy it is to be alone in the middle of a crowd. To keep things locked up inside you. To keep protecting yourself."

There. He saw a dark flash pass through Sawyer's green eyes before his friend looked back at the ocean.

"I know what happened to you," Ren said quietly. "You have to remember you survived."

At that moment, Halle looked up and caught Ren's gaze. She smiled at him, and he smiled back.

"That's in the past," Sawyer said, tone flat.

"Just... If you meet her, the right one, she'll help you. She'll pour glue in all the cracks. She'll make you feel whole again. You just have to let her in. I'm speaking from experience, here."

Sawyer just grunted.

Ren sipped his drink and watched Halle clink her glass against Sammy's. He hoped his friend got the message.

Because if he did, good things were waiting for him.

Six months later

WITH HER WETSUIT dangling at her waist, Halle finished making the coffees in the mess of the *Atalanta.* She added extra cream and sugar to Ren's.

Banging and crashing came from the galley. She raised her voice. "Good morning, Chef."

There was a pause in the banging, then a grunt. "*Dobroye utro,* Halle."

Smiling, she headed outside to find her man.

Her fiancé.

She held her hand up and the ring on her finger glinted in the morning sunlight. Ridiculous happiness filled her.

It was an oval diamond surrounded by a ring of small aquamarine stones. Blue like the water she loved. He'd done a good job. She adored it.

Ren had proposed a few weeks ago on the bow of the *Atalanta.* They'd been huddled under blankets, looking at the stars. He'd given her cotton candy, that he'd once again gotten Chef Petrov to make, and the ring had been hidden inside. She'd almost eaten it.

She sighed. It had been perfect. Ren had even called her father to get his blessing.

Her dad had come around to the idea of her and Ren as a couple. He was happy for them.

They were planning a long engagement so she could finish her studies.

"Hi, Halle," Damien called out as she passed him on the stairs.

"Have you seen Ren?"

"He's giving the new crew members a hard time on the main deck." Damien flashed her a smile.

Halle continued down to the main deck. She'd left the Navy project. She hadn't wanted to work on anything that would make her a target again. She was finishing her postgraduate work on a different project aboard the *Atalanta*.

She loved it. Being out at sea, swimming in the ocean during the day, and sleeping in bed with Ren every night. It was her idea of heaven.

"I want this deck cleaned until it shines," Ren ordered. "Rogers, get the storeroom organized and everything stowed where it belongs. Masry, I want the new submersible, *Jack*, cleaned until you can see your reflection in it."

"You got it, Ren."

He stood there wearing his navy-blue polo shirt and tan cargo shorts. Heat curled in her belly. God, her man was hot.

The new crew members all scurried off with nods.

Ren turned and spied her. His gaze ran over her bikini top. It was white today.

"Good morning, Ms. Bradshaw."

"Mr. Santoro." She handed him his coffee.

He took a sip, then set it down on a crate. "You know it drives me crazy seeing you in those bikinis."

She smiled. "I know."

He growled and pulled her in for a kiss. It turned hot, their tongues tangling.

He took her mug and set it down beside his. Then he lifted her off her feet.

"*Ren*." She clutched his shoulders.

He carried her into the lab and slammed the door

closed. It wasn't currently being used on this trip. He yanked her wetsuit down to midthigh, then set her on the edge of one of the benches. His hand slid under her bikini bottoms.

She gasped, and lifted her hips.

"There's my sexy Halle." He slid a finger inside her.

"*Ren*, I need you," she gasped. She tore at his shorts while she kicked off her wetsuit.

He shoved the cups of her bikini top down and her breasts spilled out. She opened her legs.

He opened his shorts and pulled his hard cock out. "I need you too, baby. Always." He shifted between her thighs.

The next second, he thrust inside her.

She moaned.

"Can't get enough," he gritted out. "Never enough. It always feels so right."

She stroked her hands down his back. "Because I'm yours. I was made for you."

He started thrusting—hard and fast. The pleasure built, filling every space inside her. She felt fiery sparks ignite in her belly.

"Look at me, baby," he demanded. "Look at me while I'm loving you."

She met those sexy, brown eyes. They weren't as dark and conflicted as they'd once been. These last few months, she'd seen happiness and contentment on his face so much more.

And she'd keep loving him until the old, hurtful memories were just that, memories.

"Love my Halle." He pumped into her, his muscular

body straining against hers. "Now I want to watch you come."

She felt his hand between their bodies. He found her clit and rubbed.

She scratched her nails down his back. "*Ren.*"

Halle came hard, intense pleasure coursing through her. He kept thrusting inside her, moving faster.

Then he slammed deep and poured himself inside her with a low groan.

Riding the waves of pleasure, she turned her head and kissed his neck.

They both caught their breath.

Lazily, she ran her lips over his salty skin. "*Mmm.*"

His lips found hers. "I really like your bikini."

She smiled. "I could tell."

He rubbed his thumb over her ring, his brown gaze moving over her face. "I can't wait until you're mine, in all ways."

She pressed her palm flat against his chest. She felt his heart beating steadily. "I'm already yours, Ren. I have been since you kissed me on my 20th birthday. I can't wait until you're my husband, but you already have my heart."

He'd had it for a long time. And she never wanted it back.

"And you have mine." He leaned back. "Now, I think you have some dolphins to swim with. I saw a pod earlier."

"And maybe some sharks." She slipped down off the bench and pulled her bikini back into place, then shimmied her wetsuit back up to her waist. "We picked up the trackers of some good specimens in the vicinity."

Ren froze. "No. No swimming with sharks."

"We'll see." She threw her arms around his neck. "Have I told you how much I love you?"

"Yes, but that's still a no to the sharks, Halle."

With a heart full of love, she laughed and kissed her man. She knew that wherever they went, he'd love her and keep her safe.

And she'd return the favor. She'd love him unconditionally, and keep his heart safe.

I hope you enjoyed Ren and Halle's story!

Unbroken Heroes continues with *The Hero She Deserves*, starring loner deputy sheriff Sawyer Lane. Coming late 2024/early 2025.

If you'd like to know more about **Vander Norcross** and his team, then check out the first Norcross Security book, *The Investigator*. **Read on for a preview of the first chapter.**

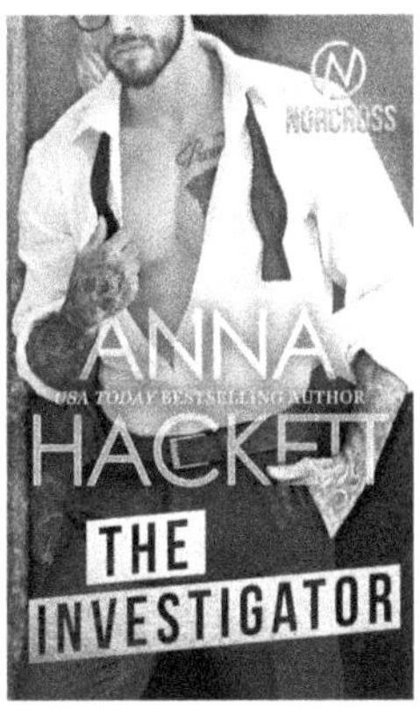

Don't miss out! For updates about new releases, free books, and other fun stuff, sign up for my VIP mailing list and get your *free box set* containing three action-packed romances.

Visit here to get started: www.annahackett.com

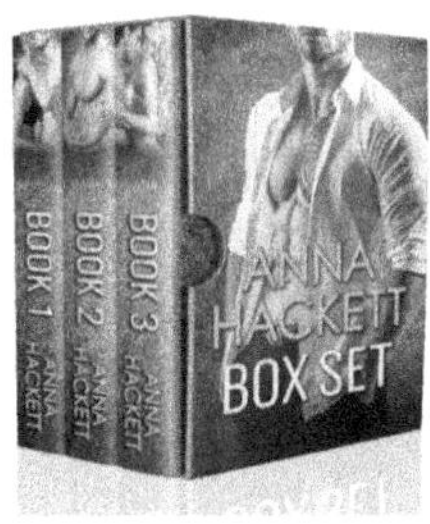

Would you like a FREE BOX SET of my books?

PREVIEW: THE INVESTIGATOR

There was a glass of chardonnay with her name on it waiting for her at home.

Haven McKinney smiled. The museum was closed, and she was *done* for the day.

As she walked across the East gallery of the Hutton Museum, her heels clicked on the marble floor.

God, she loved the place. The creamy marble that made up the flooring and wrapped around the grand pillars was gorgeous. It had that hushed air of grandeur that made her heart squeeze a little every time she stepped inside. But more than that, the amazing art the Hutton housed sang to the art lover in her blood.

Snagging a job here as the curator six months ago had been a dream come true. She'd been at a low point in her life. Very low. Haven swallowed a snort and circled a stunning white-marble sculpture of a naked, reclining woman with the most perfect resting bitch face. She'd never guessed that her life would come crashing down at age twenty-nine.

She lifted her chin. Miami was her past. The Hutton and San Francisco were her future. No more throwing caution to the wind. She had a plan, and she was sticking to it.

She paused in front of a stunning exhibit of traditional Chinese painting and calligraphy. It was one of their newer exhibits, and had been Haven's brainchild. Nearby, an interactive display was partially assembled. Over the next few days, her staff would finish the installation. Excitement zipped through Haven. She couldn't wait to have the touchscreens operational. It was her passion to make art more accessible, especially to children. To help them be a part of it, not just look at it. To learn, to feel, to enjoy.

Art had helped her through some of the toughest times in her life, and she wanted to share that with others.

She looked at the gorgeous old paintings again. One portrayed a mountainous landscape with beautiful maple trees. It soothed her nerves.

Wine would soothe her nerves, as well. *Right.* She

needed to get upstairs to her office and grab her handbag, then get an Uber home.

Her cell phone rang and she unclipped it from the lanyard she wore at the museum. "Hello?"

"Change of plans, girlfriend," a smoky female voice said. "Let's go out and celebrate being gorgeous, successful, and single. I'm done at the office, and believe me, it has been a *grueling* day."

Haven smiled at her new best friend. She'd met Gia Norcross when she joined the Hutton. Gia's wealthy brother, Easton Norcross, owned the museum, and was Haven's boss. The museum was just a small asset in the businessman's empire. Haven suspected Easton owned at least a third of San Francisco. Maybe half.

She liked and respected her boss. Easton could be tough, but he valued her opinions. And she loved his bossy, take-charge, energetic sister. Gia ran a highly successful PR firm in the city, and did all the PR and advertising for the Hutton. They'd met not long after Haven had started work at the museum.

After their first meeting, Gia had dragged Haven out to her favorite restaurant and bar, and the rest was history.

"I guess making people's Instagram look pretty and not staged is hard work," Haven said with a grin.

"Bitch." Gia laughed. "God, I had a meeting with a businessman caught in...well, let's just say he and his assistant were *not* taking notes on the boardroom table."

Haven felt an old, unwelcome memory rise up. She mentally stomped it down. "I don't feel sorry for the cheating asshole, I feel sorry for whatever poor shmuck got more than they were paid for when they walked into the boardroom."

"Actually, it was the cheating businessman's wife."

"Uh-oh."

"And the assistant was male," Gia added.

"Double uh-oh."

"Then said cheater comes to my PR firm, telling me to clean up his mess, because he's thinking he might run for governor one day. I mean, I'm good, but I can't wrangle miracles."

Haven suspected that Gia had verbally eviscerated the man and sent him on his way. Gia Norcross had a sharp tongue, and wasn't afraid to use it.

"So, grueling day and I need alcohol. I'll meet you at ONE65, and the first drink is on me."

"I'm pretty wiped, Gia—"

"Uh-uh, no excuses. I'll see you in an hour." And with that, Gia was gone.

Haven clipped her phone to her lanyard. Well, it looked like she was having that chardonnay at ONE65, the six-story, French dining experience Gia loved. Each level offered something different, from patisserie, to bistro and grill, to bar and lounge.

Haven walked into the museum's main gallery, and her blood pressure dropped to a more normal level. It was her favorite space in the museum. The smell of wood, the gorgeous lights gleaming overhead, and the amazing paintings combined to create a soothing room. She smoothed her hands down her fitted, black skirt. Haven was tall, at five foot eight, and curvy, just like her mom had been. Her boobs, currently covered by a cute, white blouse with a tie around her neck, weren't much to write home about, but she had to buy her skirts one size bigger. She sighed. No matter how much she walked or jogged —*blergh*, okay, she didn't jog much—she still had an ass.

Even in her last couple of months in Miami, when stress had caused her to lose a bunch of weight due to everything going on, her ass hadn't budged.

Memories of Miami—and her douchebag-of-epic-proportions-ex—threatened, churning like storm clouds on the horizon.

Nope. She locked those thoughts down. She was *not* going there.

She had a plan, and the number one thing for taking back and rebuilding her life was *no* men. She'd sworn off anyone with a Y chromosome.

She didn't need one, didn't want one, she was D-O-N-E, done.

She stopped in front of the museum's star attraction. Claude Monet's *Water Lilies*.

Haven loved the impressionist's work. She loved the colors, the delicate strokes. This one depicted water lilies and lily pads floating on a gentle pond. His paintings always made an impact, and had a haunting, yet soothing feel to them.

It was also worth just over a hundred million dollars.

The price tag still made her heart flutter. She'd put a business case to Easton, and they'd purchased the painting three weeks ago at auction. Haven had planned out the display down to the rivets used on the wood. She'd thrown herself into the project.

Gia had put together a killer marketing campaign,

and Haven had reluctantly been interviewed by the local paper. But it had paid off. Ticket sales to the museum were up, and everyone wanted to see *Water Lilies*.

Footsteps echoed through the empty museum, and she turned to see a uniformed security guard appear in the doorway.

"Ms. McKinney?"

"Yes, David? I was just getting ready to leave."

"Sorry to delay you. There's a delivery truck at the back entrance. They say they have a delivery of a Zadkine bronze."

Haven frowned, running through the next day's schedule in her head. "That's due tomorrow."

"It sounds like they had some other deliveries nearby and thought they'd squeeze it in."

She glanced at her slim, silver wristwatch, fighting back annoyance. She'd had a long day, and now she'd be late to meet Gia. "Fine. Have them bring it in."

With a nod, David disappeared. Haven pulled out her phone and quickly fired off a text to warn Gia that she'd be late. Then Haven headed up to her office, and checked her notes for tomorrow. She had several calls to make to chase down some pieces for a new exhibit she wanted to launch in the winter. There were some restoration quotes to go over, and a charity gala for her art charity to plan. She needed to get down into the storage rooms and see if there was anything they could cycle out and put on display.

God, she loved her job. Not many people would get excited about digging around in dusty storage rooms, but Haven couldn't wait.

She made sure her laptop was off and grabbed her handbag. She slipped her lanyard off and stuffed her phone in her bag.

When she reached the bottom of the stairs, she heard a strange noise from the gallery. A muffled pop, then a thump.

Frowning, she took one step toward the gallery.

Suddenly, David staggered through the doorway, a splotch of red on his shirt.

Haven's pulse spiked. *Oh God, was that blood?* "David—"

"Run." He collapsed to the floor.

Fear choking her, she kicked off her heels and spun. She had to get help.

But she'd only taken two steps when a hand sank into her hair, pulling her neat twist loose, and sending her brown hair cascading over her shoulders.

"Let me go!"

She was dragged into the main gallery, and when she lifted her head, her gut churned.

Five men dressed in black, all wearing balaclavas, stood in a small group.

No...oh, no.

Their other guard, Gus, stood with his hands in the air. He was older, former military. She was shoved closer toward him.

"Ms. McKinney, you okay?" Gus asked.

She managed a nod. "They shot David."

"I kn—"

"No talking," one man growled.

Haven lifted her chin. "What do you want?" There was a slight quaver in her voice.

The man who'd grabbed her glared. His cold, blue eyes glittered through the slits in his balaclava. Then he ignored her, and with the others, they turned to face the *Water Lilies*.

Haven's stomach dropped. *No.* This couldn't be happening.

A thin man moved forward, studying the painting's gilt frame with gloved hands. "It's wired to an alarm."

Blue Eyes, clearly the group's leader, turned and aimed the gun at Gus' barrel chest. "Disconnect it."

"No," the guard said belligerently.

"I'm not asking."

Haven held up her hands. "Please—"

The gun fired. Gus dropped to one knee, pressing a hand to his shoulder.

"No!" she cried.

The leader stepped forward and pressed the gun to the older man's head.

"No." Haven fought back her fear and panic. "Don't hurt him. I'll disconnect it."

Slowly, she inched toward the painting, carefully avoiding the thin man still standing close to it. She touched the security panel built in beside the frame, pressing her palm to the small pad.

A second later, there was a discreet beep.

Two other men came forward and grabbed the frame.

She glanced around at them. "You're making a mistake. If you know who owns this museum, then you know you won't get away with this." Who would go up against the Norcross family? Easton, rich as sin, had a lot of connections, but his brother, Vander... Haven suppressed a shiver. Gia's middle brother might be hot, but he scared the bejesus out of Haven.

Vander Norcross, former military badass, owned Norcross Security and Investigations. His team had put in the high-tech security for the museum.

No one in their right mind wanted to go up against Vander, or the third Norcross brother who also worked with Vander, or the rest of Vander's team of badasses.

"Look, if you just—"

The blow to her head made her stagger. She blinked, pain radiating through her face. Blue Eyes had back-handed her.

He moved in and hit her again, and Haven cried out, clutching her face. It wasn't the first time she'd been hit. Her douchebag ex had hit her once. That was the day she'd left him for good.

But this was worse. Way worse.

"Shut up, you stupid bitch."

The next blow sent her to the floor. She thought she heard someone chuckle. He followed with a kick to her ribs, and Haven curled into a ball, a sob in her throat.

Her vision wavered and she blinked. Blue Eyes crouched down, putting his hand to the tiles right in front of her. Dizziness hit her, and she vaguely took in the freckles on the man's hand. They formed a spiral pattern.

"No one talks back to me," the man growled. "Especially a woman." He moved away.

She saw the men were busy maneuvering the painting off the wall. It was easy for two people to move.

She knew its exact dimensions—eighty by one hundred centimeters.

No one was paying any attention to her. Fighting through the nausea and dizziness, she dragged herself a few inches across the floor, closer to the nearby pillar. A pillar that had one of several hidden, high-tech panic buttons built into it.

When the men were turned away, she reached up and pressed the button.

Then blackness sucked her under.

HAVEN SAT on one of the lovely wooden benches she'd had installed around the museum. She'd wanted somewhere for guests to sit and take in the art.

She'd never expected to be sitting on one, holding a melting ice pack to her throbbing face, and staring at the empty wall where a multi-million-dollar masterpiece should be hanging. And she definitely didn't expect to be doing it with police dusting black powder all over the museum's walls.

Tears pricked her eyes. She was alive, her guards were hurt but alive, and that was what mattered. The police had questioned her and she'd told them everything she could remember. The paramedics had checked her over and given her the ice pack. Nothing was broken, but she'd been told to expect swelling and bruising.

David and Gus had been taken to the hospital. She'd been assured the men would be okay. Last she'd heard, David was in surgery. Her throat tightened. *Oh, God.*

What was she going to tell Easton?

Haven bit her lip and a tear fell down her cheek. She hadn't cried in months. She'd shed more than enough tears over Leo after he'd gone crazy and hit her. She'd left Miami the next day. She'd needed to get away from her ex and, unfortunately, despite loving her job at a classy Miami art gallery, Leo's cousin had owned it. Alyssa had been the one who had introduced them.

Haven had learned a painful lesson to not mix business and pleasure.

She'd been done with Leo's growing moodiness, outbursts, and cheating on her and hitting her had been the last straw. *Asshole.*

She wiped the tear away. San Francisco was as far from Miami as she could get and still be in the continental US. This was supposed to be her fresh new start.

She heard footsteps—solid, quick, and purposeful. Easton strode in.

He was a tall man, with dark hair that curled at the collar of his perfectly fitted suit. Haven had sworn off men, but she was still woman enough to appreciate her boss' good looks. His mother was Italian-American, and she'd passed down her very good genes to her children.

Like his brothers, Easton had been in the military, too, although he'd joined the Army Rangers. It showed in his muscled body. Once, she'd seen his shirt sleeves rolled up when they'd had a late meeting. He had some interesting ink that was totally at odds with his sophisticated-businessman persona.

His gaze swept the room, his jaw tight. It settled on her and he strode over.

"Haven—"

"Oh God, Easton. I'm so sorry."

He sat beside her and took her free hand. He squeezed her cold fingers, then he looked at her face and cursed.

She hadn't been brave enough to look in the mirror, but she guessed it was bad.

"They took the *Water Lilies*," she said.

"Okay, don't worry about it just now."

She gave a hiccupping laugh. "Don't worry? It's worth a hundred and ten *million* dollars."

A muscle ticked in his jaw. "You're okay, and that's the main thing. And the guards are in serious but stable condition at the hospital."

She nodded numbly. "It's all my fault."

Easton's gaze went to the police, and then moved back to her. "That's not true."

"I let them in." Her voice broke. God, she wanted the marble floor to crack and swallow her.

"Don't worry." Easton's face turned very serious. "Vander and Rhys will find the painting."

Her boss' tone made her shiver. Something made her suspect that Easton wanted his brothers to find the men who'd stolen the painting more than recovering the priceless piece of art.

She licked her lips, and felt the skin on her cheek tug. She'd have some spectacular bruises later. *Great. Thanks, universe.*

Then Easton's head jerked up, and Haven followed his gaze.

A man stood in the doorway. She hadn't heard him

coming. Nope, Vander Norcross moved silently, like a ghost.

He was a few inches over six feet, had a powerful body, and radiated authority. His suit didn't do much to tone down the sense that a predator had stalked into the room. While Easton was handsome, Vander wasn't. His face was too rugged, and while both he and Easton had blue eyes, Vander's were dark indigo, and as cold as the deepest ocean depths.

He didn't look happy. She fought back a shiver.

Then another man stepped up beside Vander.

Haven's chest locked. *Oh, no. No, no, no.*

She should have known. He was Vander's top investigator. Rhys Matteo Norcross, the youngest of the Norcross brothers.

At first glance, he looked like his brothers—similar build, muscular body, dark hair and bronze skin. But Rhys was the youngest, and he had a charming edge his brothers didn't share. He smiled more frequently, and his shaggy, thick hair always made her imagine him as a rock star, holding a guitar and making girls scream.

Haven was also totally, one hundred percent in lust with him. Any time he got near, he made her body flare to life, her heart beat faster, and made her brain freeze up. She could barely talk around the man.

She did *not* want Rhys Norcross to notice her. Or talk to her. Or turn his soulful, brown eyes her way.

Nuh-uh. No way. She'd sworn off men. This one should have a giant warning sign hanging on him. *Watch out, heartbreak waiting to happen.*

Rhys had been in the military with Vander. Some

hush-hush special unit that no one talked about. Now he worked at Norcross Security—apparently finding anything and anyone.

He also raced cars and boats in his free time. The man liked to go fast. Oh, and he bedded women. His reputation was legendary. Rhys liked a variety of adventures and experiences.

It was lucky Haven had sworn off men.

Especially when they happened to be her boss' brother.

And especially, especially when they were also her best friend's brother.

Off limits.

She saw the pair turn to look her and Easton's way.

Crap. Pulse racing, she looked at her bare feet and red toenails, which made her realize she hadn't recovered her shoes yet. They were her favorites.

She felt the men looking at her, and like she was drawn by a magnet, she looked up. Vander was scowling. Rhys' dark gaze was locked on her.

Haven's traitorous heart did a little tango in her chest.

Before she knew what was happening, Rhys went down on one knee in front of her.

She saw rage twist his handsome features. Then he shocked her by cupping her jaw, and pushing the ice pack away.

They'd never talked much. At Gia's parties, Haven purposely avoided him. He'd never touched her before, and she felt the warmth of him singe through her.

His eyes flashed. "It's going to be okay, baby."

Baby?

He stroked her cheekbone, those long fingers gentle.

Fighting for some control, Haven closed her hand over his wrist. She swallowed. "I—"

"Don't worry, Haven. I'm going to find the man who did this to you and make him regret it."

Her belly tightened. *Oh, God.* When was the last time anyone had looked out for her like this? She was certain no one had ever promised to hunt anyone down for her. Her gaze dropped to his lips.

He had amazingly shaped lips, a little fuller than such a tough man should have, framed by dark stubble.

There was a shift in his eyes and his face warmed. His fingers kept stroking her skin and she felt that caress all over.

Then she heard the click of heels moving at speed. Gia burst into the room.

"What the hell is going on?"

Haven jerked back from Rhys and his hypnotic touch. Damn, she'd been proven right—she was so weak where this man was concerned.

Gia hurried toward them. She was five-foot-four, with a curvy, little body, and a mass of dark, curly hair. As usual, she wore one of her power suits—short skirt, fitted jacket, and sky-high heels.

"Out of my way." Gia shouldered Rhys aside. When her friend got a look at Haven, her mouth twisted. "I'm going to *kill* them."

"Gia," Vander said. "The place is filled with cops. Maybe keep your plans for murder and vengeance quiet."

"Fix this." She pointed at Vander's chest, then at

Rhys. Then she turned and hugged Haven. "You're coming home with me."

"Gia—"

"No. No arguments." Gia held up her palm like a traffic cop. Haven had seen "the hand" before. It was pointless arguing.

Besides, she realized she didn't want to be alone. And the quicker she got away from Rhys' dark, far-too-perceptive gaze, the better.

Norcross Security

The Investigator

The Troubleshooter

The Specialist

The Bodyguard

The Hacker

The Powerbroker

The Detective

The Medic

The Protector

Also Available as Audiobooks!

PREVIEW: TREASURE HUNTER SECURITY

Want to learn more about *Treasure Hunter Security*? Check out the first book in the series, *Undiscovered*, Declan Ward's action-packed story.

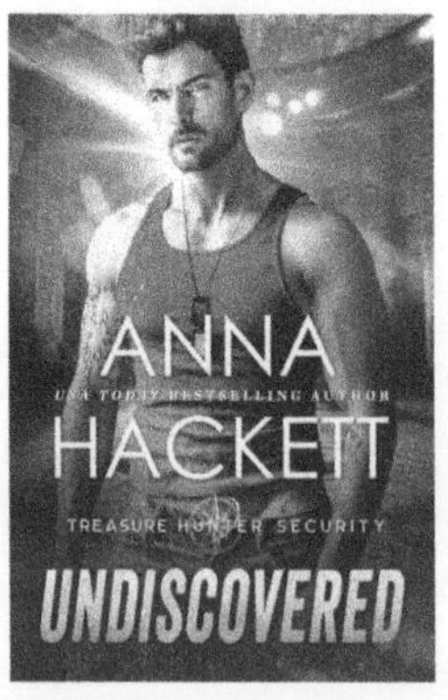

One former Navy SEAL. One dedicated archeologist. One secret map to a fabulous lost oasis.

Finding undiscovered treasures is always daring, dangerous, and deadly. Perfect for the men of Treasure Hunter Security. Former Navy SEAL Declan Ward is haunted by the demons of his past and throws everything he has into his security business—Treasure Hunter Security. Dangerous archeological digs – no problem. Daring expeditions – sure thing. Museum security for invaluable exhibits – easy. But on a simple dig in the Egyptian desert, he collides with a stubborn, smart archeologist, Dr. Layne Rush, and together they get swept into a deadly treasure hunt for a mythical lost oasis. When an evil from his past reappears, Declan vows to do anything to protect Layne.

Dr. Layne Rush is dedicated to building a successful career—a promise to the parents she lost far too young. But when her dig is plagued by strange accidents, targeted by a lethal black market antiquities ring, and artifacts are stolen, she is forced to turn to Treasure Hunter Security, and to the tough, sexy, and too-used-to-giving-orders Declan. Soon her organized dig morphs into a wild treasure hunt across the desert dunes.

Danger is hunting them every step of the way, and Layne and Declan must find a way to work together...to not only find the treasure but to survive.

Treasure Hunter Security

Undiscovered

Uncharted

Unexplored

Unfathomed

Untraveled
Unmapped
Unidentified
Undetected
Also Available as Audiobooks!

ALSO BY ANNA HACKETT

Fury Brothers

Fury

Keep

Burn

Also Available as Audiobooks!

Unbroken Heroes

The Hero She Needs

The Hero She Wants

Also Available as Audiobooks!

Sentinel Security

Wolf

Hades

Striker

Steel

Excalibur

Hex

Also Available as Audiobooks!

Norcross Security

The Investigator

The Troubleshooter

The Specialist

The Bodyguard

The Hacker

The Powerbroker

The Detective

The Medic

The Protector

Also Available as Audiobooks!

Billionaire Heists

Stealing from Mr. Rich

Blackmailing Mr. Bossman

Hacking Mr. CEO

Also Available as Audiobooks!

Team 52

Mission: Her Protection

Mission: Her Rescue

Mission: Her Security

Mission: Her Defense

Mission: Her Safety

Mission: Her Freedom

Mission: Her Shield

Mission: Her Justice

Also Available as Audiobooks!

Treasure Hunter Security

Undiscovered

Uncharted

Unexplored

Unfathomed

Untraveled

Unmapped

Unidentified

Undetected

Also Available as Audiobooks!

Oronis Knights

Knightmaster

Knighthunter

Knightqueen

Galactic Kings

Overlord

Emperor

Captain of the Guard

Conqueror

Also Available as Audiobooks!

Eon Warriors

Edge of Eon

Touch of Eon

Heart of Eon

Kiss of Eon

Mark of Eon

Claim of Eon

Storm of Eon

Soul of Eon

King of Eon

Also Available as Audiobooks!

Galactic Gladiators: House of Rone

Sentinel

Defender

Centurion

Paladin

Guard

Weapons Master

Also Available as Audiobooks!

Galactic Gladiators

Gladiator

Warrior

Hero

Protector

Champion

Barbarian

Beast

Rogue

Guardian

Cyborg

Imperator

Hunter

Also Available as Audiobooks!

Hell Squad

Marcus

Cruz

Gabe

Reed

Roth

Noah

Shaw

Holmes

Niko

Finn

Devlin

Theron

Hemi

Ash

Levi

Manu

Griff

Dom

Survivors

Tane

Also Available as Audiobooks!

The Anomaly Series

Time Thief

Mind Raider

Soul Stealer

Salvation

Anomaly Series Box Set

The Phoenix Adventures

Among Galactic Ruins

At Star's End

In the Devil's Nebula

On a Rogue Planet

Beneath a Trojan Moon

Beyond Galaxy's Edge

On a Cyborg Planet

Return to Dark Earth

On a Barbarian World

Lost in Barbarian Space

Through Uncharted Space

Crashed on an Ice World

Perma Series

Winter Fusion

A Galactic Holiday

Warriors of the Wind

Tempest

Storm & Seduction

Fury & Darkness

Standalone Titles

Savage Dragon

Hunter's Surrender

One Night with the Wolf

For more information visit www.annahackett.com

ABOUT THE AUTHOR

I'm a USA Today bestselling romance author who's passionate about ***fast-paced, emotion-filled*** contemporary romantic suspense and science fiction romance. I love writing about people overcoming unbeatable odds and achieving seemingly impossible goals. I like to believe it's possible for all of us to do the same.

I live in Australia with my own personal hero and two very busy, always-on-the-move sons.

For release dates, behind-the-scenes info, free books, and other fun stuff, sign up for the latest news here:

Website: www.annahackett.com

Milton Keynes UK
Ingram Content Group UK Ltd.
UKHW031311090824
1219UKWH00022B/50